# TUZAĞI
12 AĞUSTOS 1915

# TUZAĞI
## 12 AGUSTOS 1915

PAUL S. DOBBINS

BILL RABBIT PRESS
HERNDON, VIRGINIA

ISBN: 978-0-9983789-0-9 (PAPERBACK EDITION)

LIBRARY OF CONGRESS CONTROL NUMBER 00000000000

SOME CHARACTERS AND EVENTS IN THIS BOOK ARE FICTIONAL, ANY SIMILARITY
TO REAL PERSONS, ALIVE OR DEAD, IS COINCIDENTAL AND NOT INTENDED BY THE
AUTHOR.

EDITING BY ROBERTA CASTRO DOBBINS
FRONT COVER IMAGE BY PAUL S. DOBBINS
BOOK DESIGN BY PAUL S. DOBBINS

PRINTED AND BOUND IN THE U.S.A.
FIRST PRINTING, AUGUST 2017

PUBLISHED BY PAUL S. DOBBINS
1325 FORTY OAKS DRIVE
HERNDON, VA 20170-2024

*FOR MY WONDERFUL BERTIE*
*WITH LOVE*

**_TUZAGI_ IS TURKISH FOR TRAP**


TU  zAH  EE
[G IS "SILENT"]

(JUST BETWEEN YOU AND ME, THE AUTHOR SAYS _TAZOWIE_)

# CONTENTS

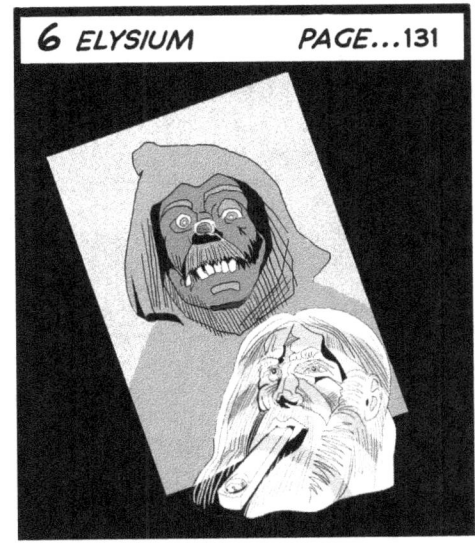

# ACKNOWLEDGMENTS

FROM START TO FINISH *TUZAGI* HAS BEEN A LONG LABOR OF LOVE. LOVE AND LEARNING. THAT LOVE ENTAILS THE EFFORT PUT INTO *TUZAGI'S* CREATION, AND THE RESPECT, ENCOURAGEMENT, ADVICE AND INTEREST OTHERS HAVE OFFERED IN SUPPORT OF THE PROJECT.

FIRST AND FOREMOST IS MY WIFE ROBERTA, WHO NATURALLY AND WILLINGLY BORE THE BRUNT OF LIVING WITH ANOTHER'S OBSESSION FOR MANY A LONG MONTH, STRETCHING INTO YEARS. MY CHILDREN, NOAH AND KATE, WERE ALSO THERE, FAR AND NEAR TO ADD THEIR SUPPORT. KATE PROVIDED SOME VERY POINTED CRITICISM EARLY ON, AFTER REVIEWING EARLY STORYBOARDS, THAT MOTIVATED GREATER EFFORT ON MY PART TO BRING THE ART UP TO A HIGHER STANDARD. THERE MAY BE MUCH MORE ROOM FOR IMPROVEMENT ALONG THOSE LINES, BUT THE ART NOW CARRIES THE STORY AND THE LESSONS LEARNED WILL CARRY OVER INTO FUTURE PROJECTS.

I LEARNED MUCH FROM READING MANY "HOW TO BOOKS" ON THE SUBJECTS OF SEQUENTIAL ART AND GRAPHIC NOVEL DESIGN AND DEVELOPMENT. SOME OF THE BEST OF THESE ARE LISTED UNDER *REFERENCES* AT THE END OF THE BOOK. IN PARTICULAR, FREDDIE WILLIAMS II ON DIGITAL DRAWING METHODS IN PHOTOSHOP™, SHAWN MARTINBROUGH ON COMIC NOIR, AND JOHN LOWE ON WORKING METHODS. ARTISTS WHO HAVE TAUGHT (PERHAPS MUCH TO THEIR SURPRISE), ENTERTAINED AND INSPIRED ME INCLUDE THE LEGENDARY JOE KUBERT, STEVE RUDE THE DUDE OF *NEXUS* FAME, ERIC SHANOWER AND HIS AMAZING *AGE OF BRONZE* SERIES, AND MIKE MIGNOLA AND *HELLBOY.* THERE ARE MANY NAMES I WOULD ADD TO THE LIST, BUT LET'S MEET AT THE BAR AND TALK ABOUT IT.

MANY FRIENDS HAD A CHANCE TO VIEW THE ART IN SOME FORM AS IT PROGRESSED FROM THUMBNAIL TO FINISH. *PRINTKEEPER!* A ROUND OF GIGLEES FOR MY FRIENDS. I THANK THEM FOR MANY COMMENTS THAT MADE A DIFFERENCE. I ALSO WANT TO THANK SEVERAL INDUSTRY PROFESSIONALS WHO TOOK A CAREFUL LOOK AT MY WORK AND OFFERED HELPFUL COMMENTS AND ENCOURAGEMENT, INCLUDING CHRIS SPAROS OF *TOP SHELF,* CHRIS PITZER OF *ADHOUSE BOOKS,* AND DIRK WOOD OF *IDW.*

# INTRODUCTION

ON APRIL 25TH, 1915, AN ENGLISH-FRENCH AMPHIBIOUS ASSAULT WAS LAUNCHED AGAINST THE NORTHERN FLANK -- GALLIPOLI -- OF THE TURKISH DARDANELLES DEFENSES. THE PURPOSE OF THE ATTACK WAS TO OPEN THE FRONT DOOR FOR A NAVAL ATTACK ON ISTANBUL BY THE OVERWHELMING POWER OF THE ALLIED FLEET. SUCH AN ATTACK, IF SUCCESSFUL, WOULD FORCE TURKEY OUT OF THE WAR AND PROVIDE SUCCOR FOR THE HARD-PRESSED RUSSIANS, THEN FIGHTING A TWO-FRONT WAR AGAINST AUSTRIA-HUNGARY AND TURKEY.

THE AMPHIBIOUS ASSAULT TARGETED TWO ZONES ON THE GALLIPOLI COAST, "HELLAS" ON THE SOUTHWEST POINT, AND WHAT CAME TO BE KNOWN AS "ANZAC", MIDWAY UP THE COAST *(PLEASE REFER TO THE MAPS INSIDE THE FRONT COVER)*.

THE UNDERPOWERED ASSAULT DID NOT GO ACCORDING TO PLAN, AND NEARLY FAILED COMPLETELY ON THE FIRST DAY, NOT IN SMALL PART DUE TO THE STOUT TURKISH DEFENSE. *AND ALLIED ERRORS!* THE ANZAC ASSAULT, FOR EXAMPLE, LANDED TOO FAR NORTH OF THE INTENDED LANDING PLACE, PUTTING THE INVADERS -- FROM THE AUSTRALIAN-NEW ZEALAND CORPS -- ON THE WRONG SIDE OF THREE FORMIDABLE, EASILY DEFENDED RIDGELINES. THE HELLAS LANDINGS, A FIVE-PRONGED ATTACK, WERE LIGHTLY OPPOSED *WHERE IT DIDN'T* MATTER (TO THE PLANNERS AND THE TACTICAL OFFICER COMMANDING, MAJOR GENERAL HUNTER-WESTON), AND BRUTALLY OPPOSED *WHERE IT DID.*

FIGHTING OVER THE FOLLOWING WEEKS DEVOLVED INTO A SERIES OF BRUTE FORCE ATTACKS AND COUNTERATTACKS. THE ALLIES WERE UNABLE TO REACH THEIR D-DAY OBJECTIVES (EVER), AND THE TURKS WERE UNABLE TO FORCE THE ALLIES OUT THEIR ENTRENCHED LOGEMENTS. THUS WAS SET IN MOTION THE PLAN FOR THE ALLIED AUGUST OFFENSIVE THROUGH SUVLA BAY, NORTH OF ANZAC, AND THE REMARKABLE TALE OF THE 1/5 NORFOLKS.

OUR STORY, HOWEVER, BEGAN SOMETIME BEFORE ENGLAND ENTERED THE GREAT WAR IN 1914. INDEED, IN 1908, EDWARD THE VII CREATED A COMPANY OF VOLUNTEERS FROM THE STAFF OF THE ROYAL ESTATE AT SANDRINGHAM. THESE MEN AND YOUTHS FARMED THE ESTATE, GROOMED AND TENDED THE HORSES, AND MAINTAINED THE GREAT HOUSE AND ITS ENVIRONS.

WHEN WAR BROKE OUT, THE KING HAD NO INTENTION OF COMMITTING THE COMPANY TO THE FIGHTING, BUT RESPONDING TO THE VOICES OF HER LOYAL SERVANTS, THE QUEEN MOTHER INTERVENED AND WON A CONCESSION FROM HER SON TO LET THE SANDRINGHAM MEN BE MEN. THE COMPANY WAS ROLLED INTO THE TERRITORIAL ARMY, BECOMING COMPANY 'E" OF THE 5TH BATTALION OF THE ROYAL NORFOLK REGIMENT.

AS SUCH, THE COMPANY CAME TO BE ASSIGNED TO THE HEAVY REINFORCEMENTS BEING SHIPPED TO GENERAL HAMILTON'S FORCE AT GALLIPOLI. TO BREAK THE DEALOCKS AT ANZAC AND HELLAS, A RENEWED EFFORT WOULD HIT THE TURKS, A.K.A. THE JOHNNIES, OR SIMPLY JACKO, ON THEIR EXPOSED RIGHT FLANK NORTH OF ANZAC, AT SUVLA BAY. *THAT IS WHERE OUR STORY OPENS......*

# PORTAL 1

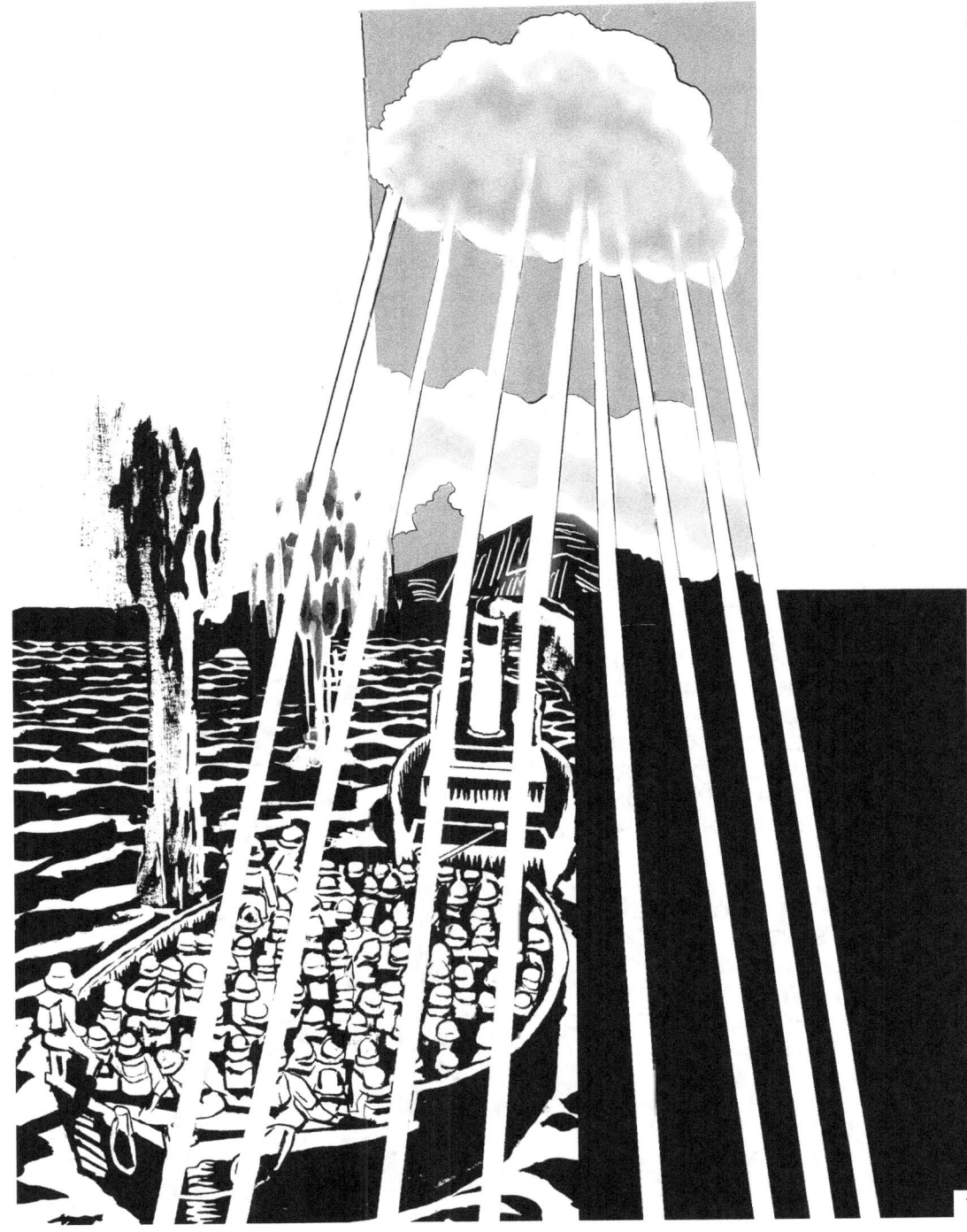

HERE I AM LIEUTENANT GEOFFREY BEGOLE-SMITH, WITH THE LADS, THE MORNING BEFORE IT STARTED, OR RATHER, ENDED. DOFFING HELMET IS MY MATE SERGEANT TOMMY BROWN. MY PLATOON IS PART OF COMPANY D, TERRITORIAL BATTALION, ROYAL NORFOLK REGIMENT.

THE STOUT LADS OF D ARE DRAWN FROM THE KING'S ESTATE AT SANDRINGHAM. MOSTLY FARMERS AND GROOMS LED BY CLERKS POSING AS NON-COMMISSIONED OFFICERS. EXCEPT ME. AM I THE SAME ROMANTIC WHO ONCE STUDIED THE CLASSICS AT *OXFORD*?

*GALLIPOLI*--THE VERY SOUND OF THAT NAME SENDS SHIVERS DOWN MY SPINE. OUR UNIT MOVED OFF THE TRANSPORT AND LOADED INTO A *BEETLE,* A LARGE FLAT BOTTOMED LIGHTER, TOWED ASHORE BY A NAVY LAUNCH.

*JACKO* DID HIS BEST TO KILL US AS WE WERE TOWED ASHORE.

3

WE LANDED AT SUVLA BAY AT 5:30 A.M.
ON AUGUST THE 10TH

THE BARGE GROUNDED IN THE SURF. WE WADED ASHORE
INTO THE HEAT, THE FLIES AND THE STINK OF GALLIPOLI

DESPITE THE HEAT, THERE WAS A CHILL IN THE AIR. IN VAIN, I ARGUE FOR CAUTION

2:05 P.M.

THE MEN ARE POORLY EQUIPPED & LACK WATER

I SHOULD HAVE PREFERRED MORE TIME. BUT I HAVE *MY ORDERS!*

4:15 P.M.

TZIP

WE STEP OFF--A SLOW ADVANCE ON THE *ANAFARTA* FRONT. *MISSION?* CLEAR SNIPERS OUT OF THE WOOD

CAPTAIN BECK'S OUTER CALM SUSTAINS US.

TOKEN RESISTANCE, THEN JACKO'S *BIG GUNS* OPEN ON US

7

SERGEANT BROWN -- *TOMMY*                    -- *IS PINNED*

**BREAKTHROUGH!** CAN'T THINK ABOUT *TOMMY NOW*

10

AS I LEARNED LATER, CAPTAIN BECK LED THE SURVIVORS OF THE COMPANY TO THE SAFETY OF A SMALL VILLA. MY PLATOON, CONFUSED BY THE SMOKE & FIRE, HAD SWANNED OFF

THEY SAID THE CLOUD SIMPLY LIFTED OFF THE GROUND TAKING US WITH IT

DID WE MOVE UP OR DOWN?

ONLOOKERS SAID, A LARGE *BREAD-SHAPED CLOUD* ENVELOPED THE COMPANY

COULDN'T *HEAR* OR *SEE*

AUSSIES SPILL OVER THE WALL. A BIG HAIRY-ASSED BASTARD, AN NCO CARRYING A WOUNDED OFFICER, MIRACULOUSLY SCALES THE WALL LIKE BILLY GOAT GRUFF. THE JOHNNIES DRAW OFF NO DOUBT SURPRISED BY OUR SUDDEN APPEARANCE.

WHERE'N'ELL YA POMMIE BASTARDS BEEN?

*EASY* SERGEANT

HE TUMBLES ASS-OVER-END OVER THE WALL, 14 DUMPING HIS BURDEN.

JUMPING TO HIS FEET, THE BIG BAS-TARD GRABS ME, OFF HIS HEAD.

MY LADS BACK HIM OFF AS I RESPOND TO THE VISE ON MY WRIST.

**HOLD** THEM, LIEUTENANT THAT'S... AN...ORDER...

*HE IS A MAJOR!*

**FUCK ORDERS,** MATE. GO TELL THE POMMIE BASTARDS WE AIN'T DYING HERE. WE'RE TAKING LYON HOME.

THEY WOULDN'T LISTEN, THEY DON'T CARE. THEY LEFT.

HOURS LATER, AFTER MEAGRE RATIONS, I NOTED THE DAY'S STRANGE EVENTS

15

AS EXPECTED, THEY STARTED COMING AT US EARLY MORNING

AFTER FICHTING FOR HOURS -- BY ANY MEANS -- WE FINALLY BROKE THEM

CLICK!
CLICK!
CLICK!

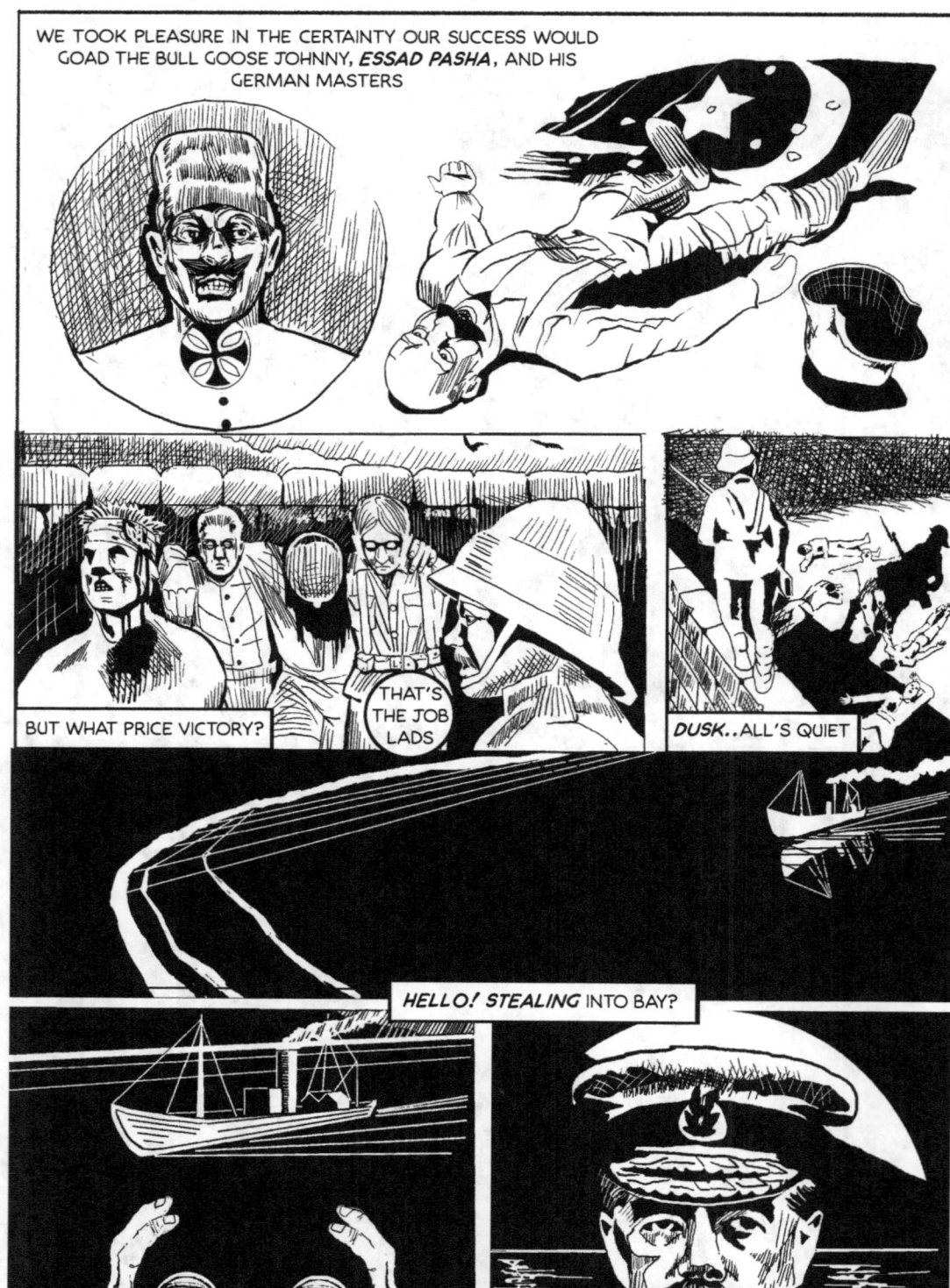

19

EARLY MORNING WE MOVED OUT INTO THE
CARNAGE. AUSSIE AND TURK SHARE THEIR
"BOUNTY", WEAPONS AND AMMO, THE
QUIET ASSENT OF THE DEAD.

SOME BADLY NEEDED AMMO, AND
MORE RIFLES TO REPLACE THOSE
BROKEN OVER JACKO'S HEAD
YESTERDAY

WELL BACK FROM THE WALL, SOME OF THE LADS TAKE A
CHANCE TO SCRUB OFF THE MUCK. IT COULD BE A SCENE
FROM A PAINTING IN A PARIS SALON.

*THEY ARE COMING....*

WITH A DESPERATE SURGE, JACKO OVERWHELMS THE DEFENSE AT THE WALL

BASTARD!

UGGHHHH!

AAIIIIEEEEEEEE!

CRACK!

THWACK!

IN THE MADNESS OF BATTLE A MAN WILL DO ANYTHING TO SURVIVE...SMASHING HEADS LIKE SO MANY *PUMPKINS.*

WE GAVE THEM ALL THEY COULD TAKE AND MORE. JACKO HAD HAD ENOUGH AS HE CLAWED HIS WAY TO SAFETY

SAHIB! THE TURKS ARE *BEHIND* YOU!

A RUNNER -- A *SIKH* SCOUT -- LOPES UP BEHIND US

CHRIST*!* WHAT IS THIS JIBBERISH?

AT LAST I *UNDERSTOOD* THE JOHNNIES HAD FOUND A PATH TO OUR REAR.

THE ASSAULT, *WITH MAXIMS,* WAS FORMING UP BEHIND US

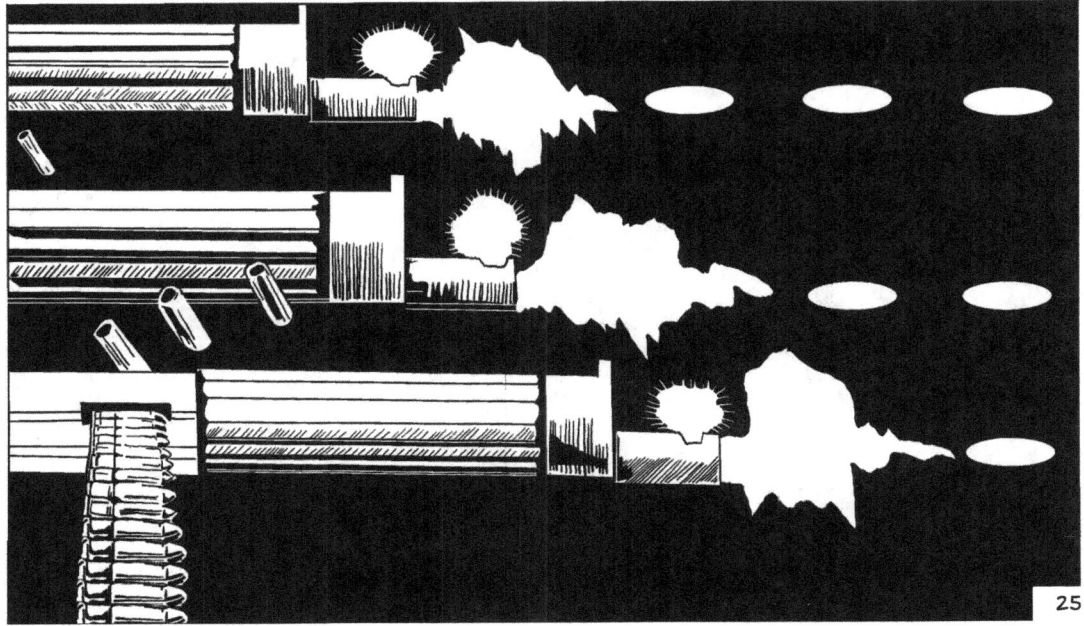

RAT TAT TAT TAT TAT TAT
TAT TAT
RAT TAT TAT TAT TAT TAT
RAT TAT TAT TAT TAT TAT
RAT TAT TAT TAT
RAT TAT TAT TAT
TAT
TAT TAT TAT TAT

# RAGE (MENIS) 2

THE GERMAN COMMANDER OF THE TURKISH DEFENSE, LIMON VON SANDERS, EXPECTED A BRITISH AT-TACK ON THE NARROW BOTTLENECK OPENNING INTO THE GALLIPOLI PENINSULA KNOWN TO HIM AS BOLAYER, A.K.A. BULAIR.

BULAIR WAS FORTIFIED BY STONE WALLS GOING BACK AT LEAST TO THE CRIMEAN WAR (1853-6). THERE ONCE WAS AN OTTO-MAN CASTLE THERE, IN THE 14TH CENTURY, AS WELL.

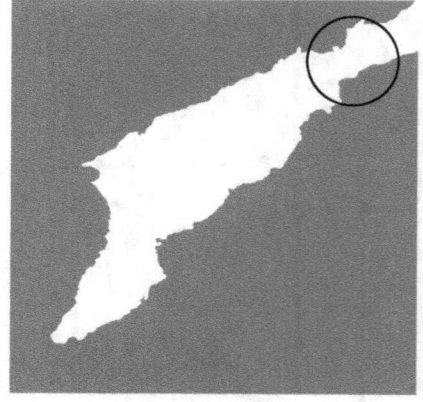

THE LAND ROUTE THROUGH PENINSULA VIA BULAIR WAS ROUGH GOING BY ANY STANDARD.

WHETHER LIEUTENANT BEGOLE-SMITH'S BRAVE LITTLE BAND OF PALS COULD HAVE MADE A DIFFERENCE BY HOLDING THE WALL, FANTASY OR NOT, WILL NEVER BE KNOWN.

PERHAPS WE JUST WITNESSED SOMETHING MORE ANCIENT, A MORE FUNDAMENTAL CONFRONTATION OF EAST AND WEST, WHICH HAS PLAYED OUT BEFORE.

## MANY TIMES........

THIS TIME, THE PALS WERE THE EXPENDABLES. WHAT NEXT?

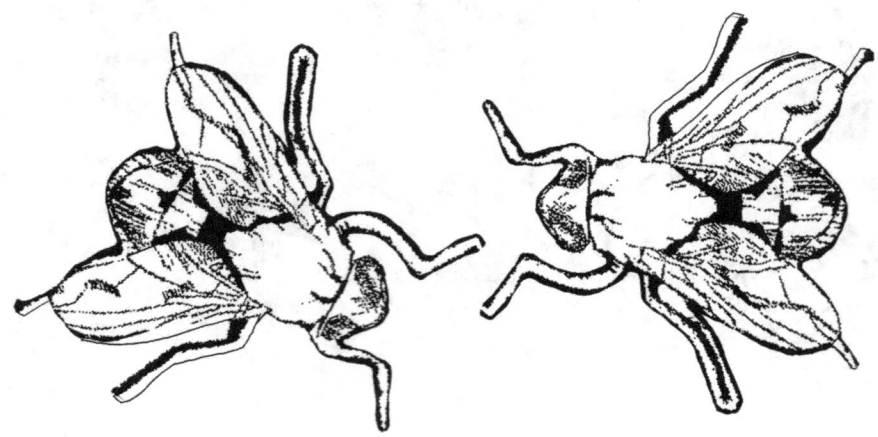

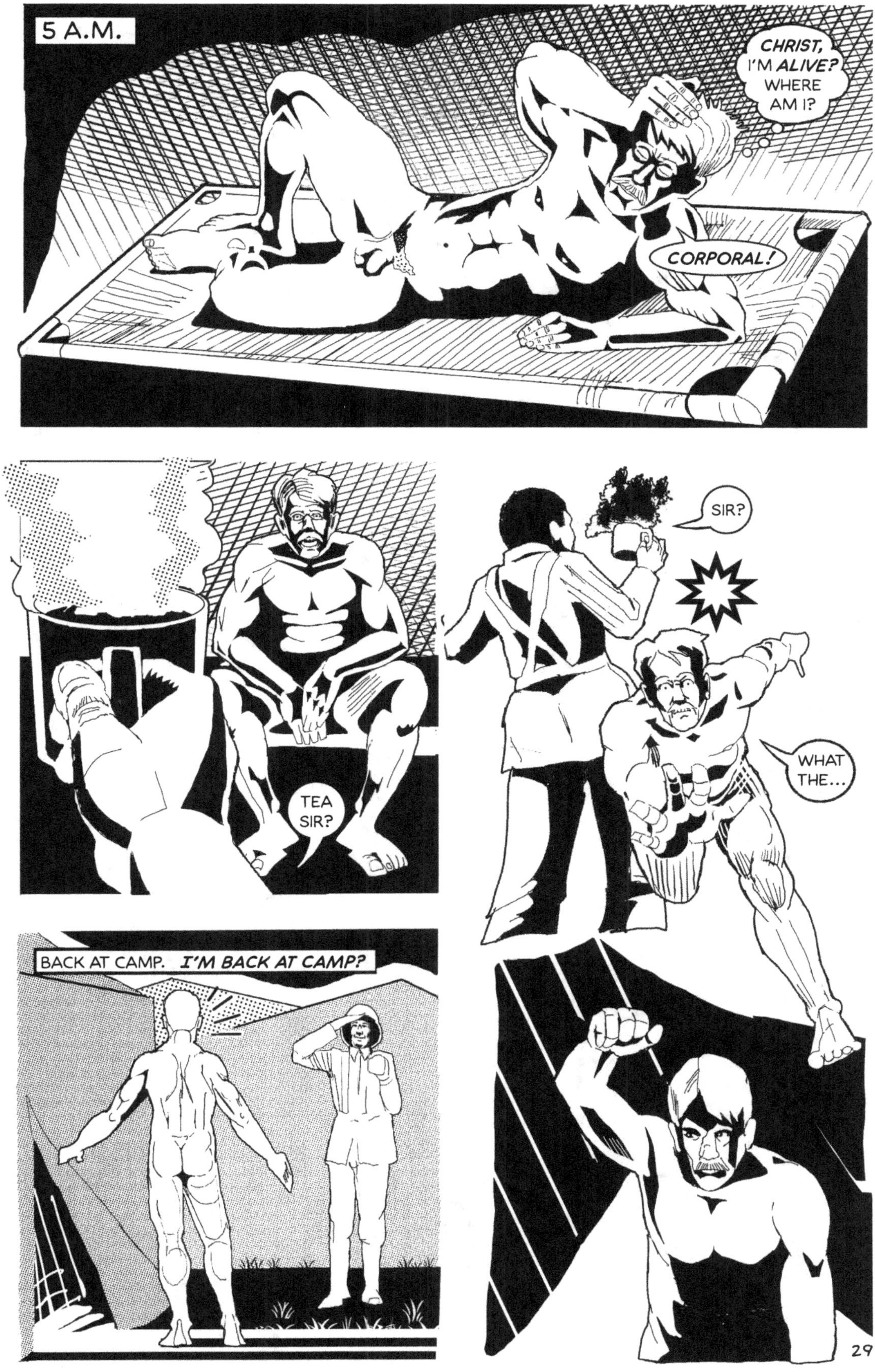

29

1:50 P.M.

2:00 P.M.

M'GOD, THIS AGAIN!

32

33

34

35

THE MAD HEADLONG RUSH UP THE SLOPE, *WEAPONLESS*, I HUNG ON TO MY NEAREST COMPANIONS AND LOST MYSELF IN THE SHEAR TERROR OF THE MOMENT

NO... IS THAT... WHAT? IT'S HIM!

*FUCKING JACKALS* WHY MUTILATE HIM? WHY TAKE HIS *EARS*?

41

43

44

ONCE WE GOT IN AMONGST THE JOHNNIES THE FIGHT WAS OVER QUICKLY. SEIZED BY BATTLE MADNESS, IN RAGE SO PURE AND HORRIFIC, I LED MY MEN ON A *NO-QUARTER-GIVEN DEATH ROMP*

KUNA LESSETERA
KUNA LESSETERA

THEIR SURVIVORS FLEE TO THE *LAST REDOUBT* THE
SUMMIT OF WHAT I LATER LEARNED IS... *HILL Q*

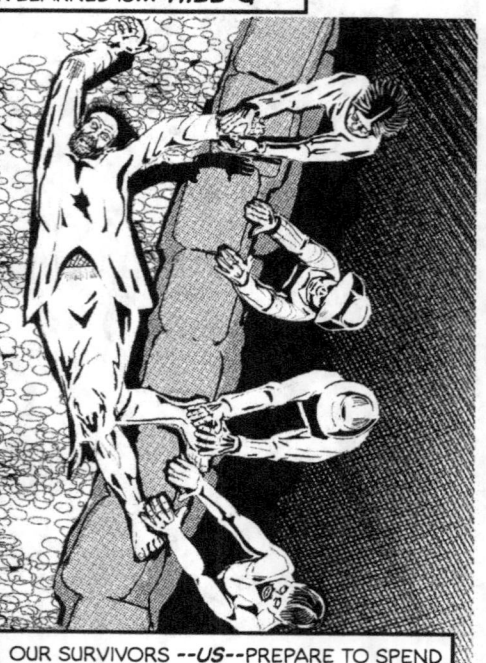

OUR SURVIVORS --*US*--PREPARE TO SPEND
THE NIGHT IN OUR HARD WON TRENCH

46

47

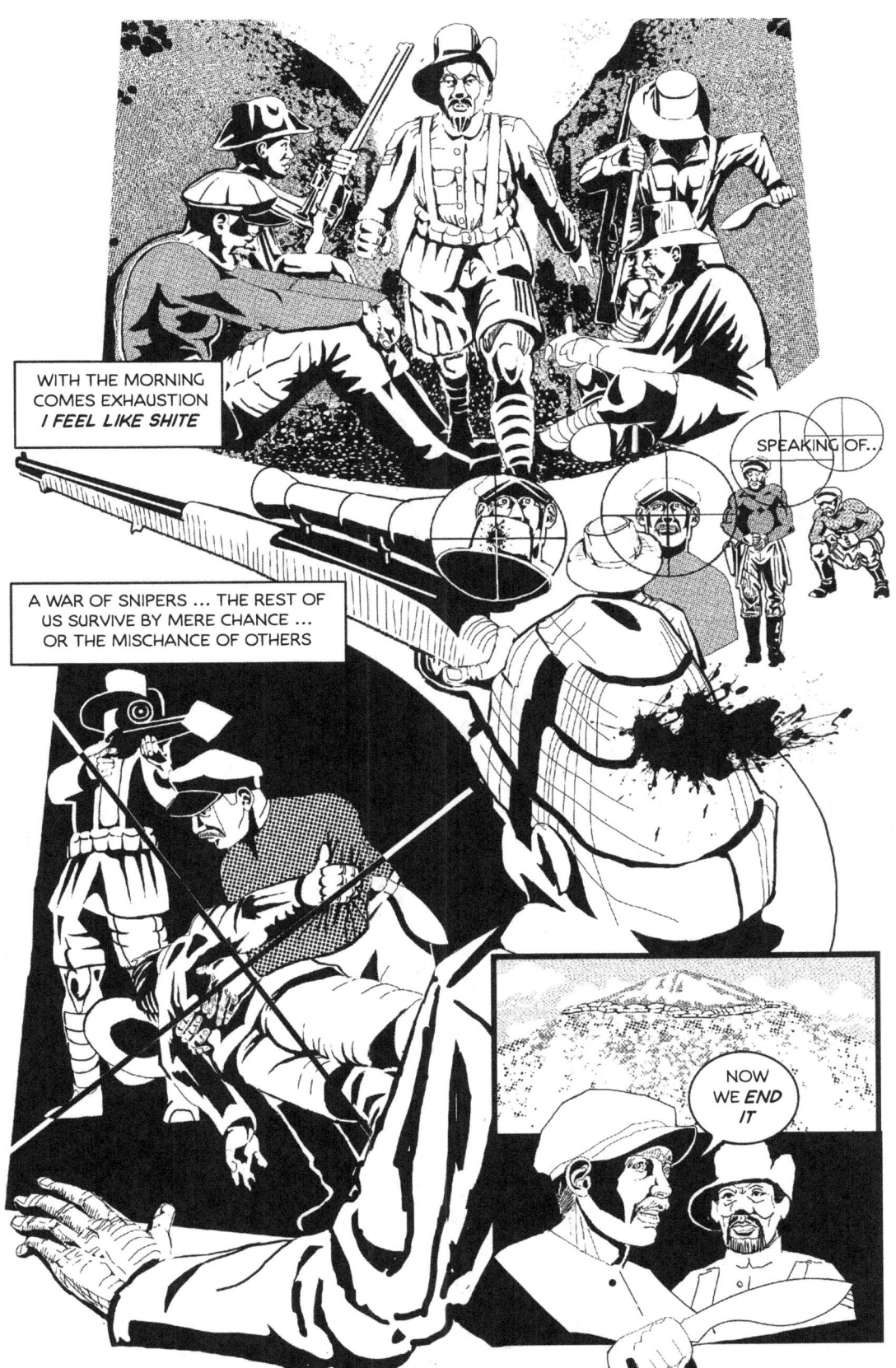

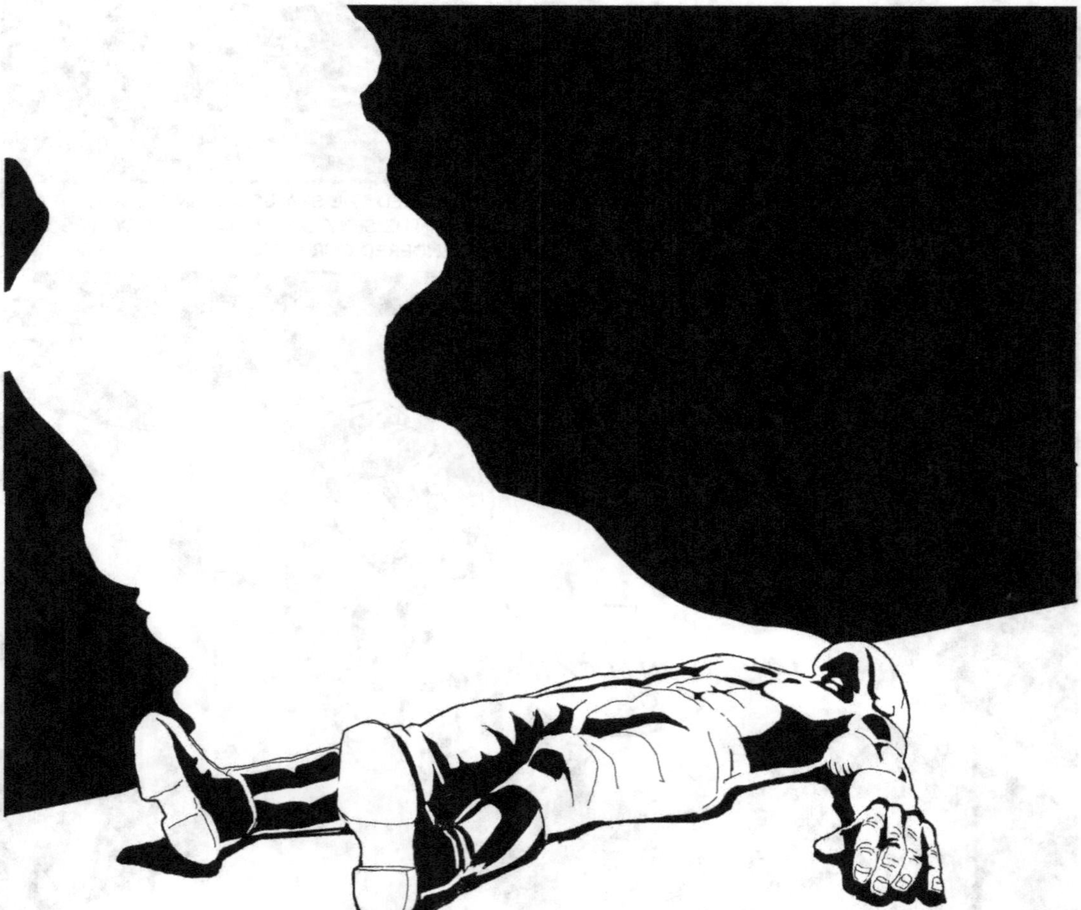

# DAPHNIS AND CHLOE 3

THERE ARE LIMITS TO WHAT THE EFFORT, HOWEVER HEROIC, OF THE INDIVIDUAL MAY ACCOMPLISH IN THE CHAOS OF WAR.

LIEUTENANT BEGOLE-SMITH, CONFUSED AND EXHAUSTED, SOUGHT TO WITHDRAW FROM THE FIGHT. IN SO DOING HE LOST A FRIEND, SERGEANT BROWN, WHOSE LIFE HE MAY HAVE SAVED. HIS ANGER, DRIVEN BY SELF LOATHING, PROPELLED HIM INTO A RAGE BEFORE WHICH ALL MUST SUCCOMB.

EXCEPT ARTILLERY, BANE OF MODERN WARFARE, WHICH INDISCRIMINANTLY BREAKS AND CASTS THE WOULD BE HERO ASIDE.

HE COULD NOT HOLD THE WALL, DEATH NOTWITHSTANDING. HE COULD NOT SAVE A FRIEND, A SOLDIER WHOSE LIFE WAS GIVEN HIM IN SACRED TRUST.

*ABIDE, GEOFFREY, ABIDE*

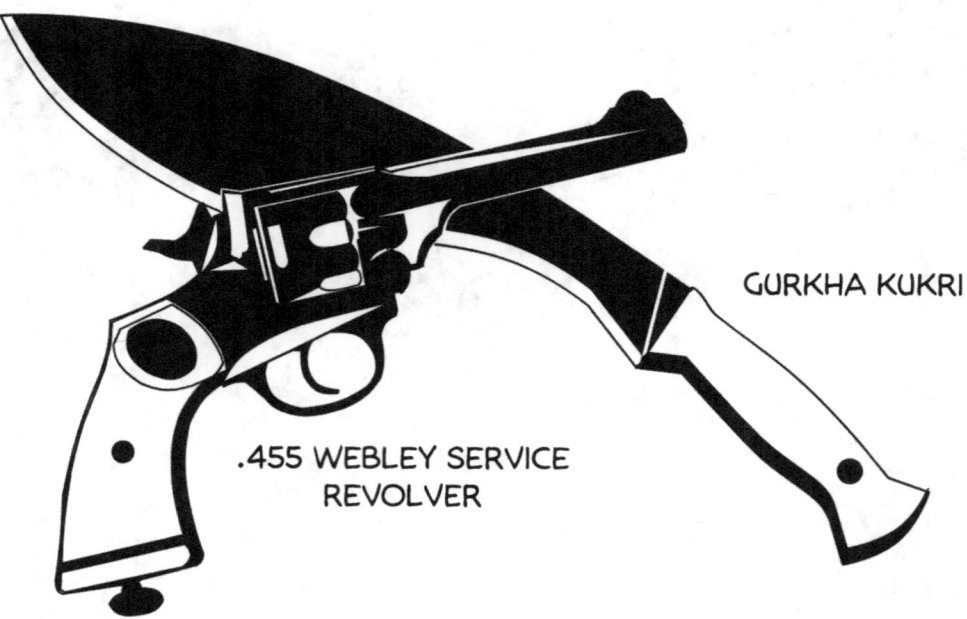

GURKHA KUKRI

.455 WEBLEY SERVICE REVOLVER

56

4:20 PM

HMMMM...SHE LOOKS FAMILIAR

FLESH WOUND I'D SAY

YIP!

SLAP

BASTARD!

EASY RELAX I'VE NOTHIN....

UGH!

61

63

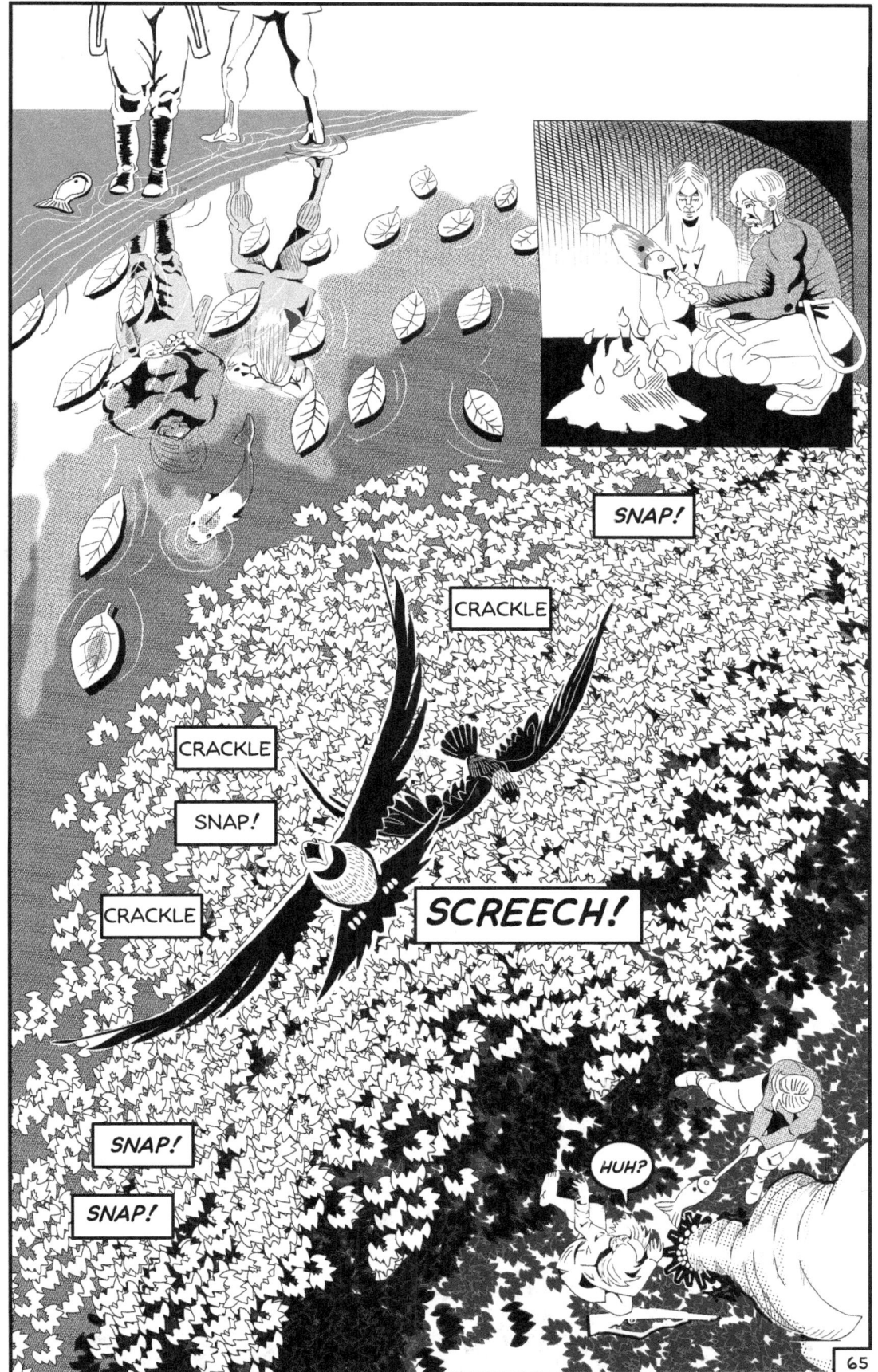

69

71

YIP YIP YIP YIP YIP YIP YIP YIP HHOOOWWWLLLLLLL

HEAD TOWARDS THE FOG

I'M NOT SURE

IF THIS WORKS, WE'LL GET BACK

77

# ODYSSEY 4

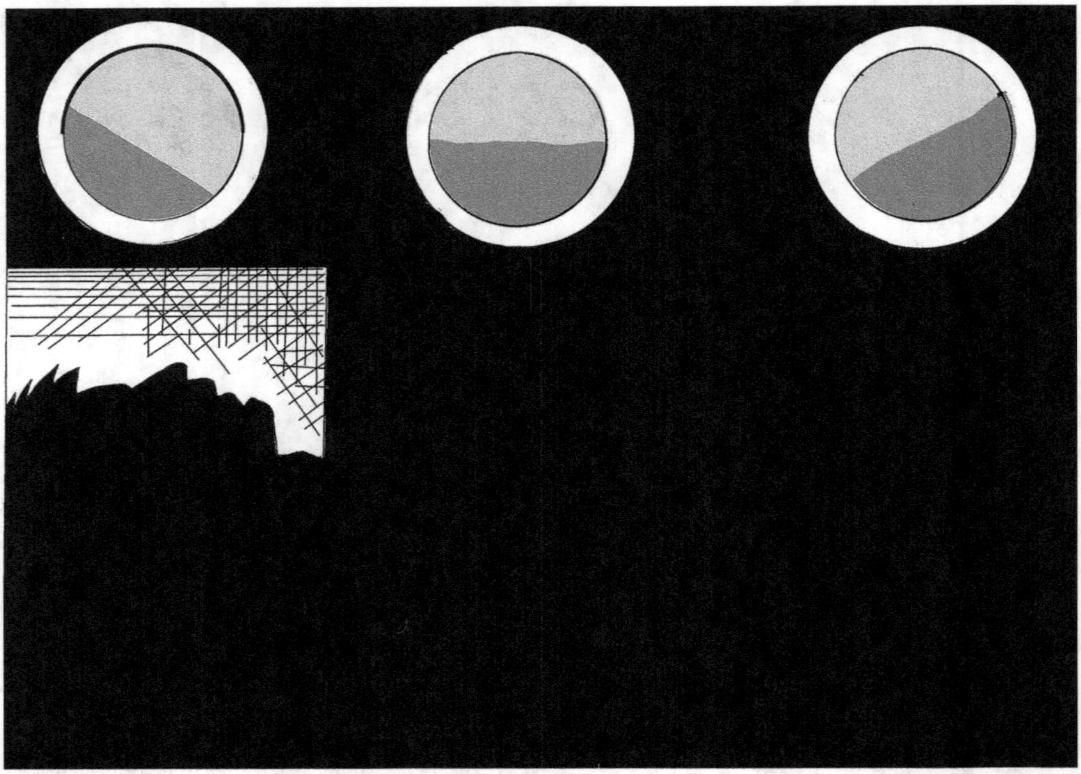

MEMORIES OF TIMES PAST, OF FRIENDS AND LOVERS, HAUNT HIM. THERE ARE CULTURAL DEMANDS, TOO, FOR SURVIVAL. THESE TRANSCEND THE PERSONAL NEEDS OF THOSE MOST DISPOSED TO GUARANTEE THEIR SURVIVAL. A MAN AND HIS LOVER.

THE MEN, HIS MEN, MAY NOT MAKE IT THROUGH THE TRIALS OF THE TIMES. BUT HIS LOVES MUST.

AND THE ENEMY MAY COME FROM WITHIN AS WELL AS FROM WITHOUT. WHERE ONCE STOOD PROUD SOLDIERS, THERE NOW STANDS JACKALS AND SCAVENGERS, WORSE THAN THE JOHNNIES.

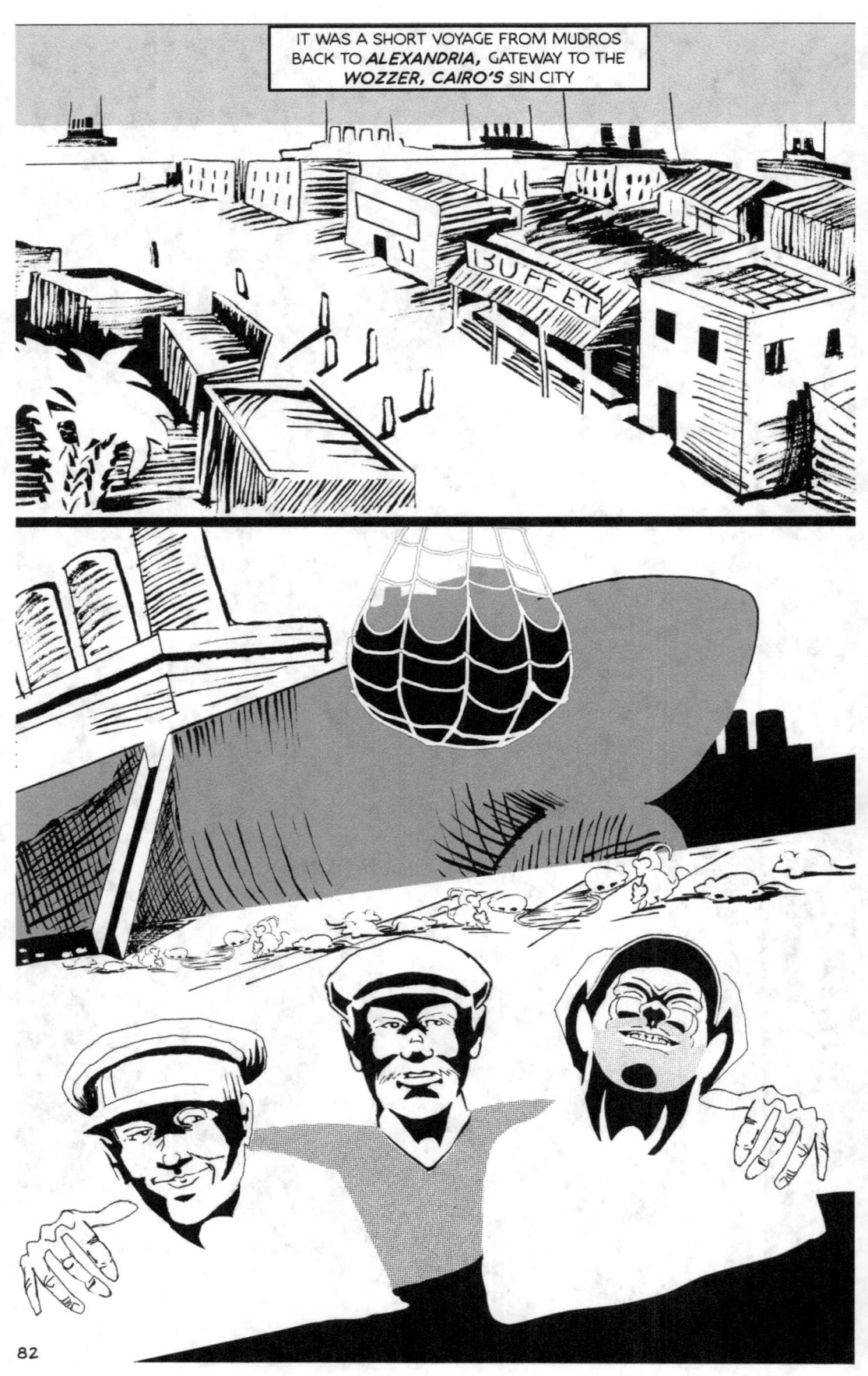

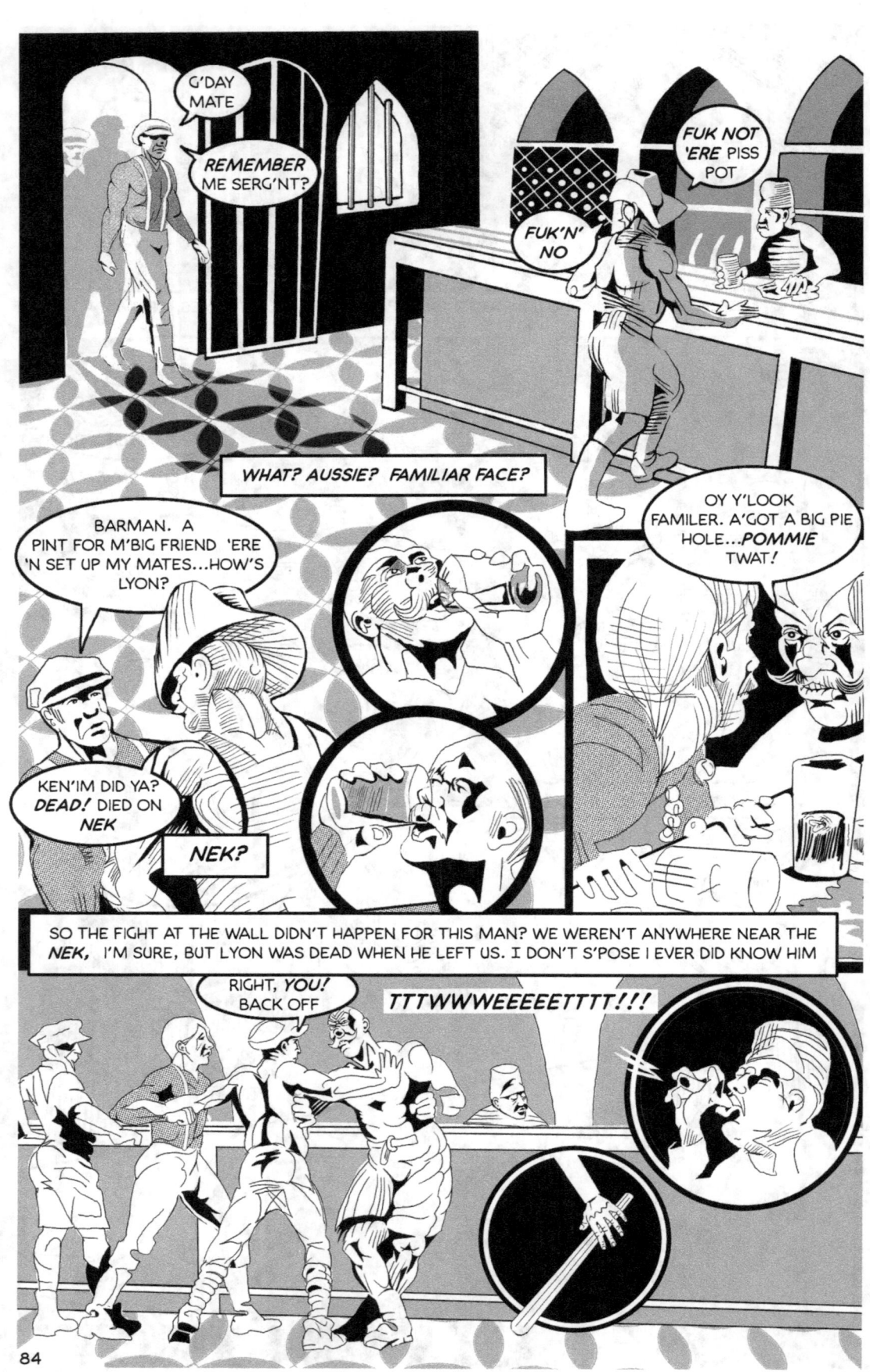

RROOOAAAARRRRR!

87

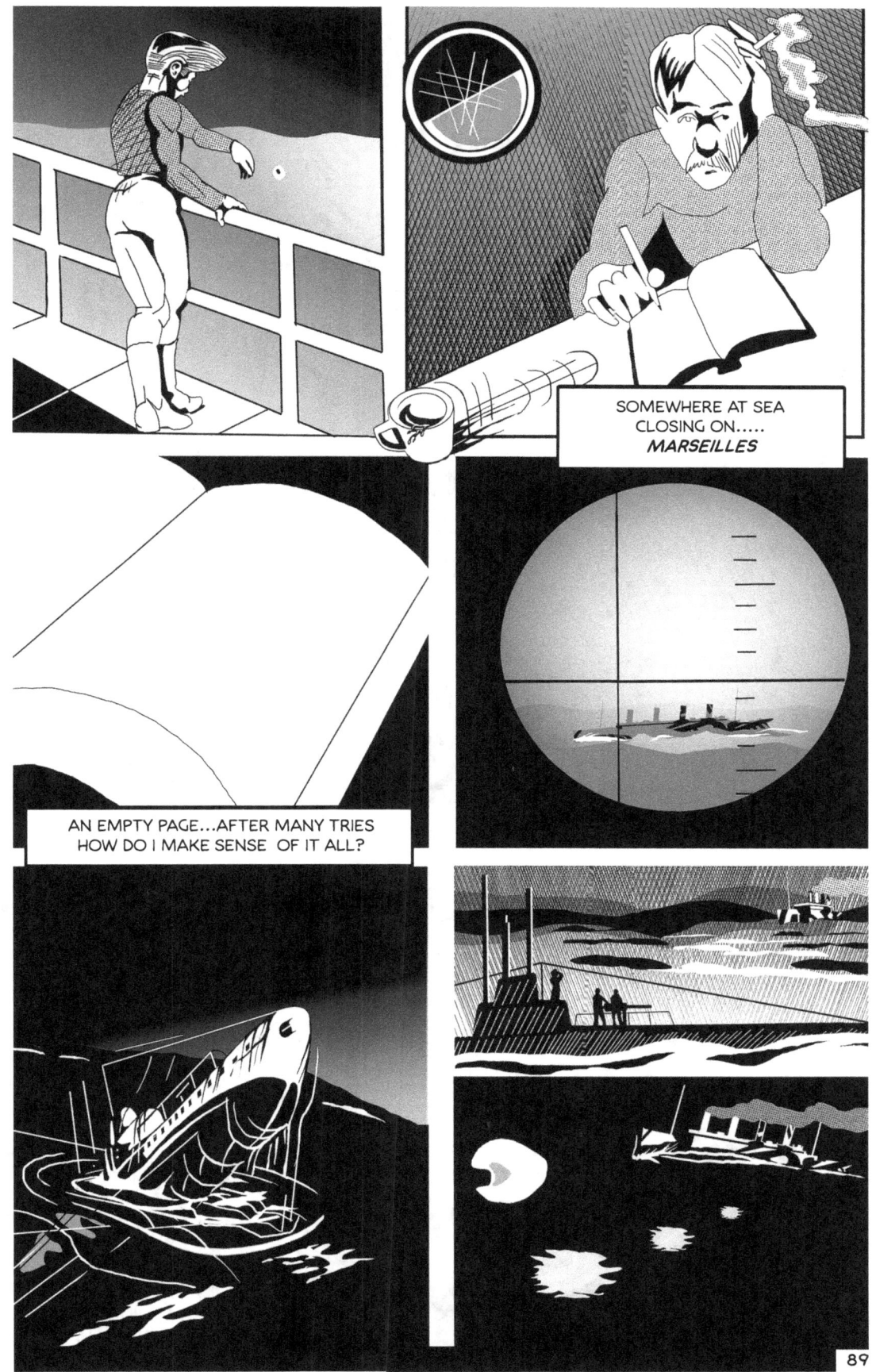

SOMEWHERE AT SEA
CLOSING ON.....
*MARSEILLES*

AN EMPTY PAGE...AFTER MANY TRIES
HOW DO I MAKE SENSE OF IT ALL?

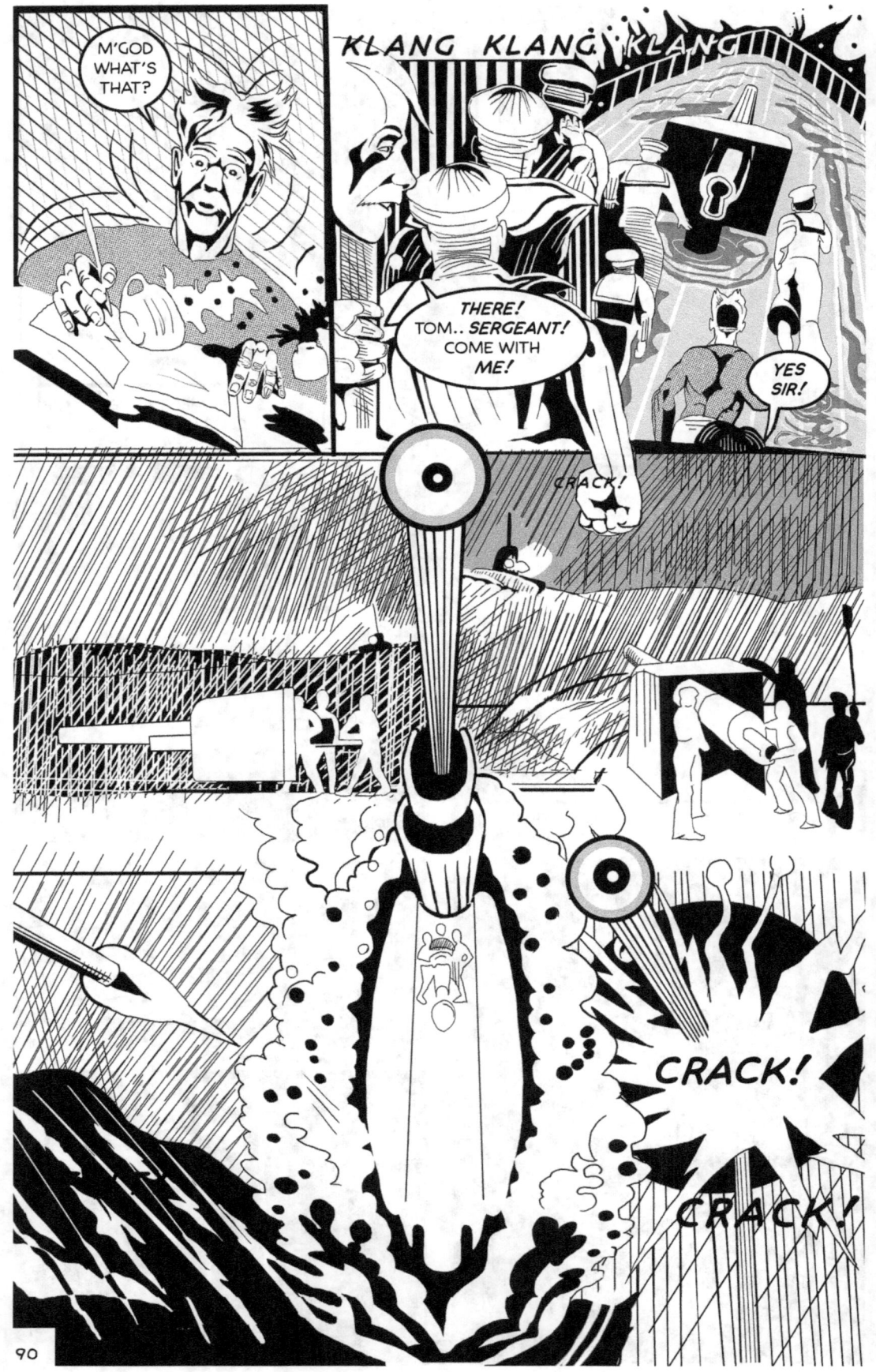

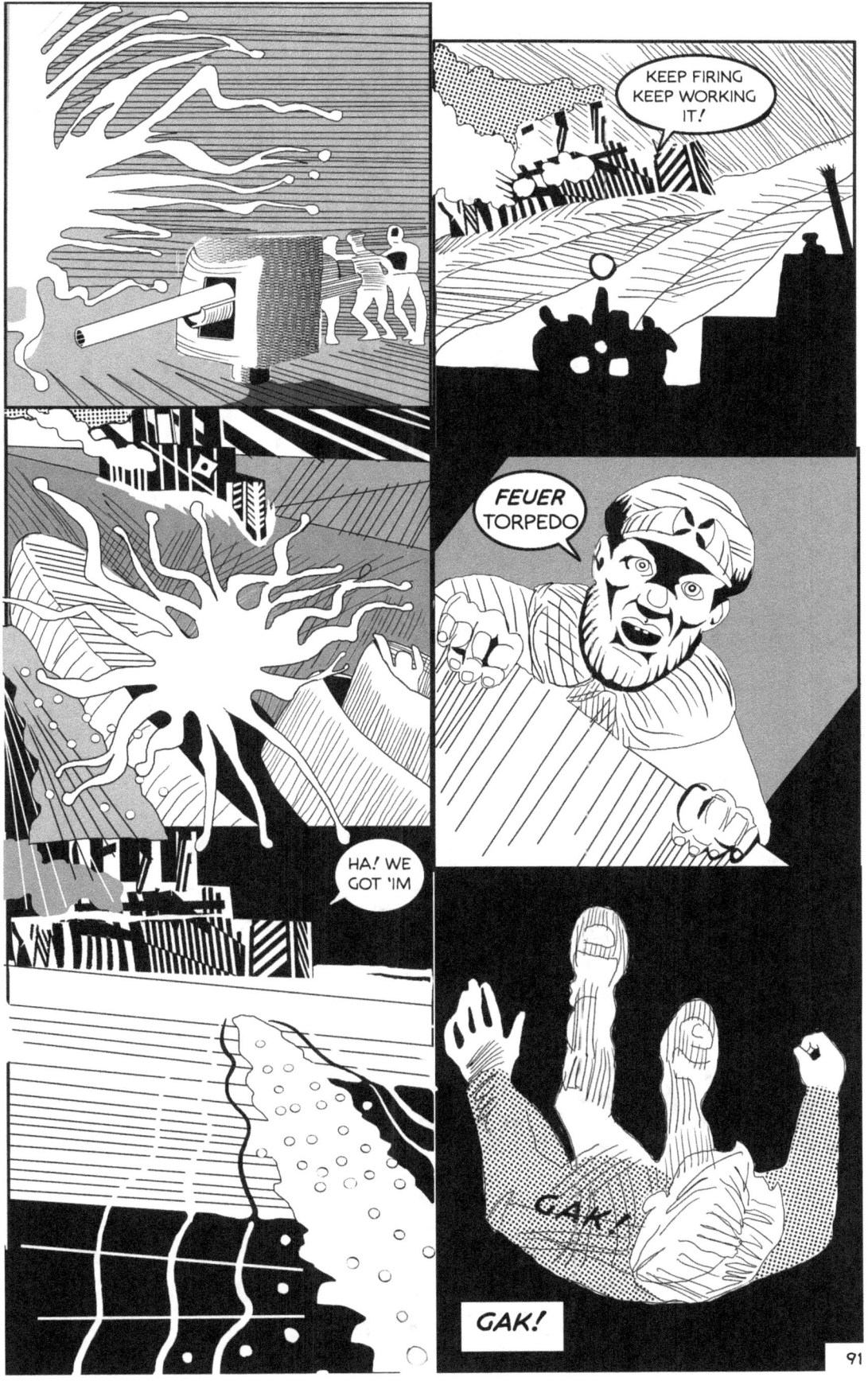

91

GASP! GLUB GLUB GASP!

NOT IN THIS LIFETIME, *BASTARDS*

HEY! ANYBODY? YYOOO OOOHHH!

94

97

98

99

101

GAS IS THE

KILLER!

GAK!

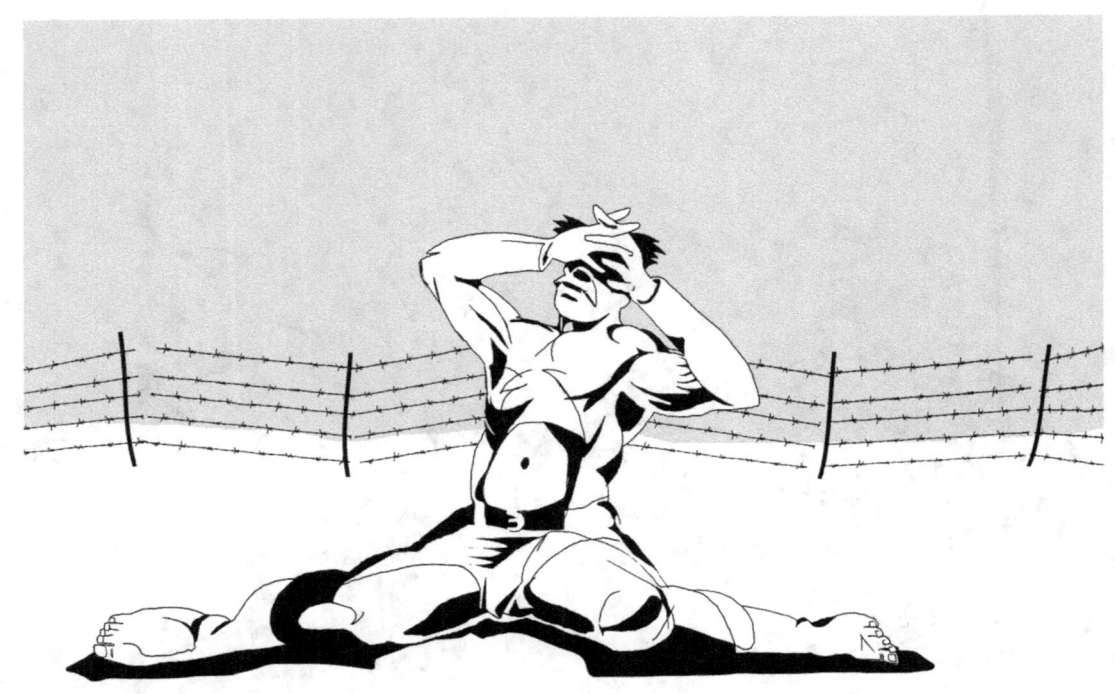

# *NOSTOS* 5
## (HOMECOMING)

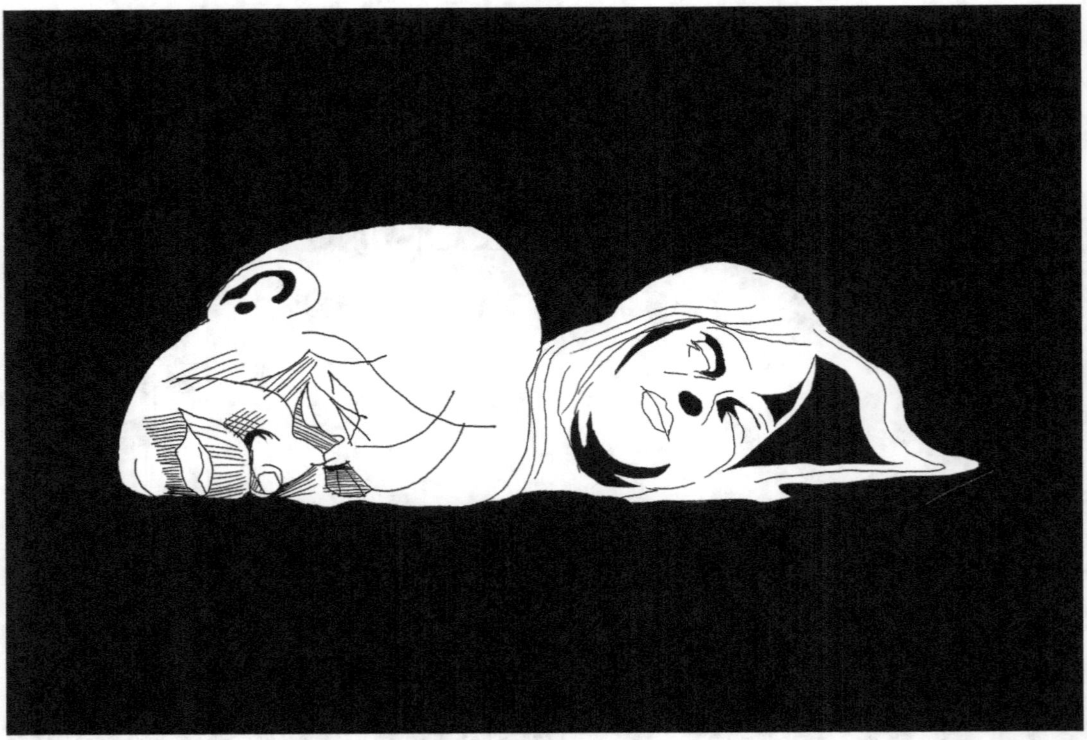

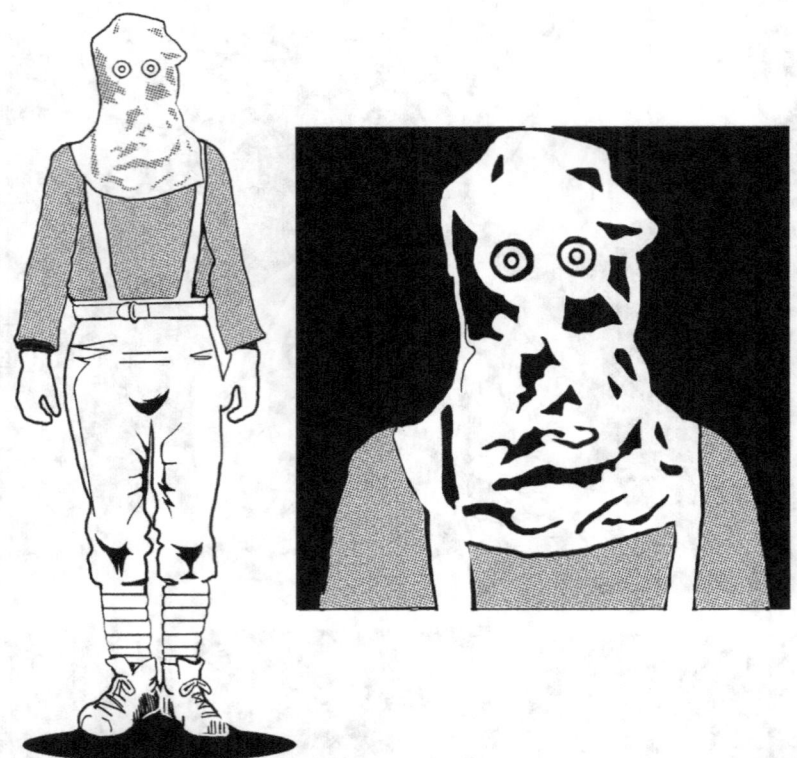

GEOFFREY BEGOLE-SMITH, LIEUTENANT OF THE SANDRINGHAM "PALS", TO A NAME-
LESS TOMMY GASSED AT YRES.  NO HEROIC LAST STAND AT WALL, NOR A GLORIOUS
DEATH AT THE SUMMIT OF A KEY ENEMY POSITION,
PERHAPS BETTER THAN DEATH BY SNIPER BULLET OR JACKALS?

NO! GAS WITHOUT A MASK .....

PLEASE COME BACK

109

WHAT SHALL WE DO TODAY?
NAUGHTY BOY!
WHAT ELSE?
I'M NOT NAUGHTY

PANT! PANT! PANT!
SOMETHING DIFFERENT?

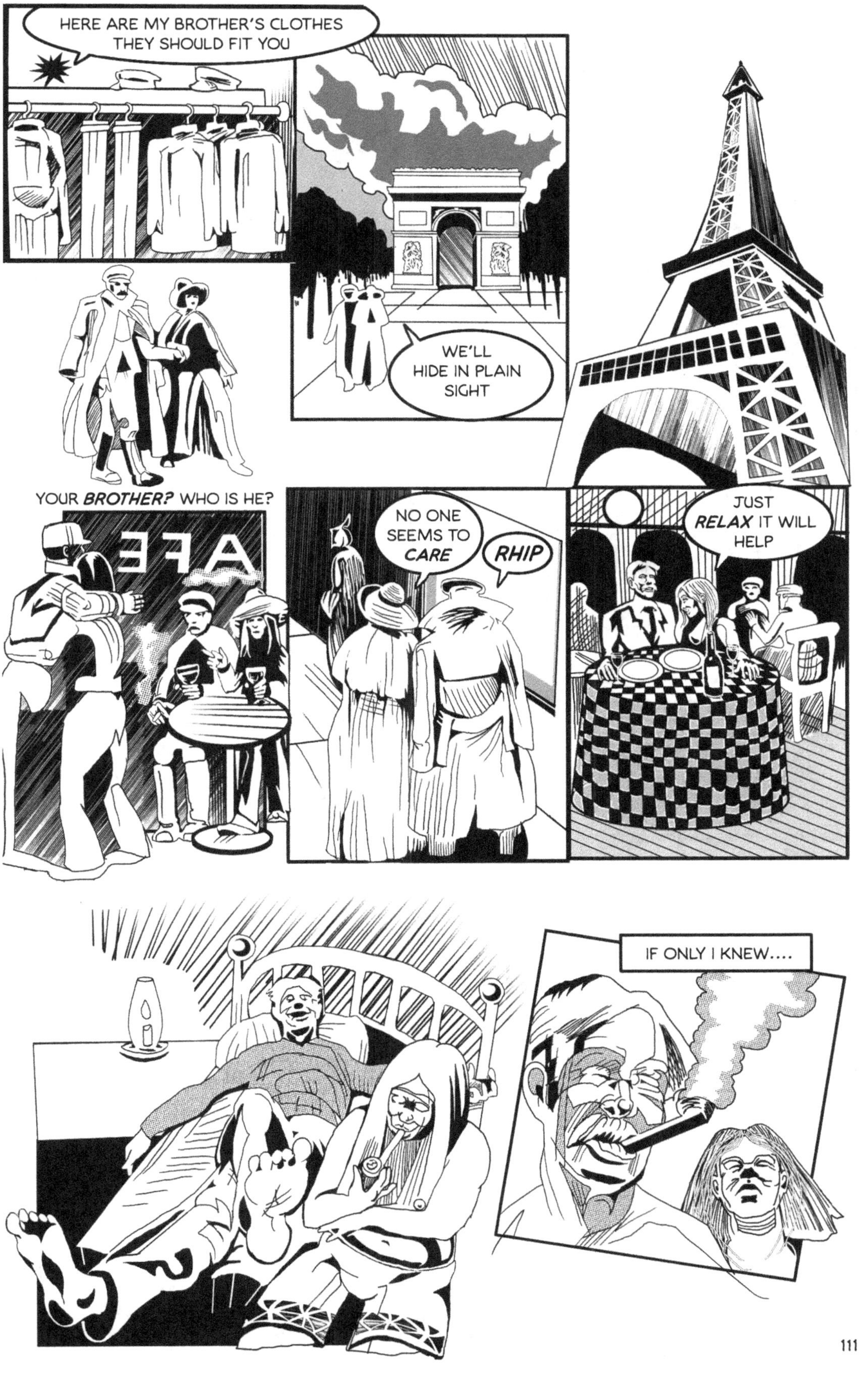

111

113

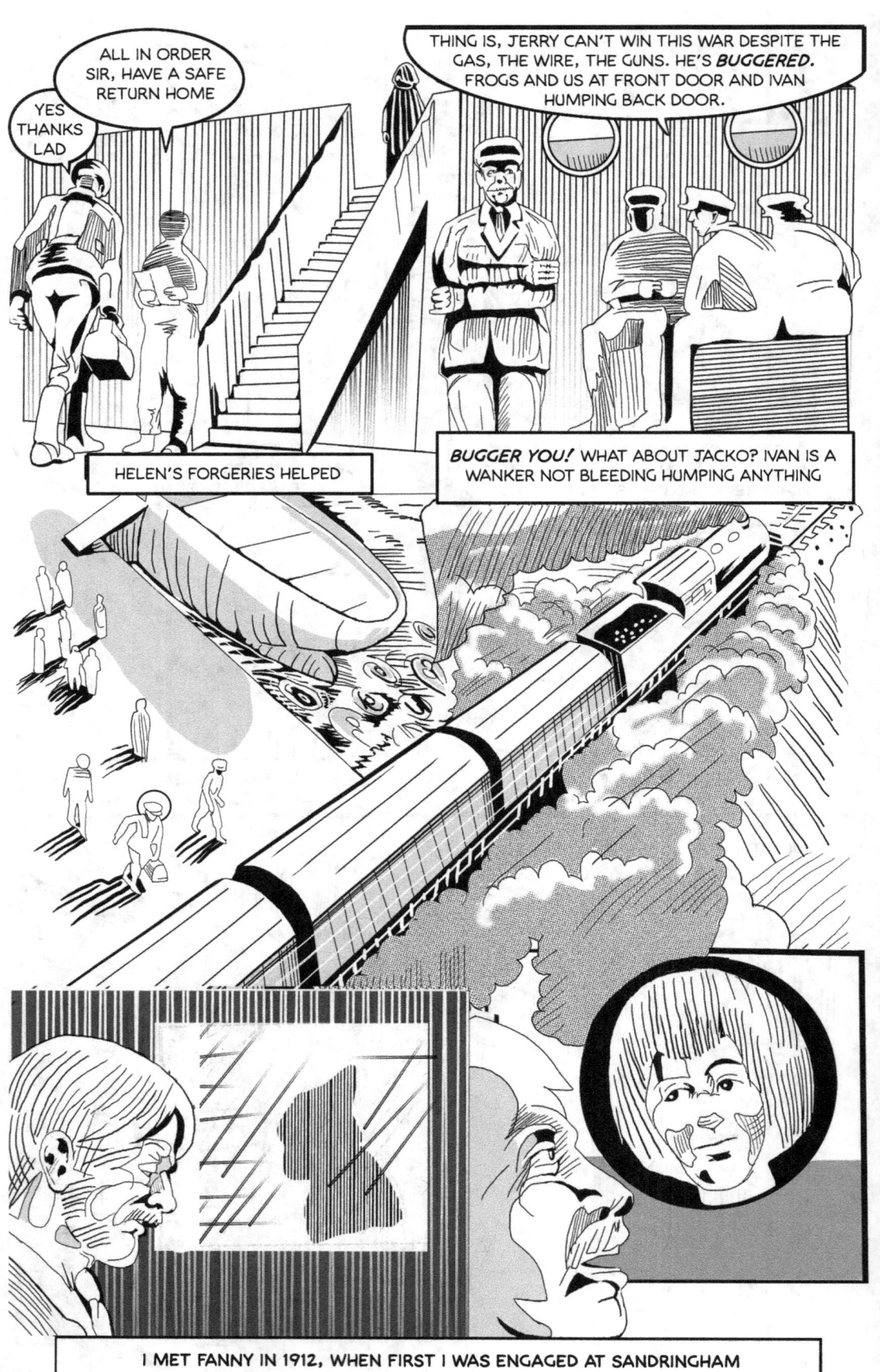

115

I, *GEOFFREY BEGOLE-SMITH*, DO TAKE *FANNY GREY* TO BE MY LAWFULY WEDDED ....ALL TOO SOON CAME A SECOND BRIDE... *WAR*

WITH THE COMING OF THE WAR, ALL THE SANDRINGHAM MEN, THE *PALS* THEY CALLED US, JOINED UP TO FORM *COMPANY E, 1ST BATTALION, 5TH NORFOLK REGIMENT.*

IT BEGINS-*OR ENDS*-NOW

I'M NOT COMING HOME THROUGH THE *FRONT DOOR*

I MAY BE A *FUGITIVE* WHO KNOWS?

BE MORE COMFORTABLE HAVING A LOOK SEE FROM *THE BUSH* AS IT WERE

119

120

124

125

OOOOOWWWLLLL
HHOOWWLLL!

EXHAUSTED
*IT'S OVER!*

127

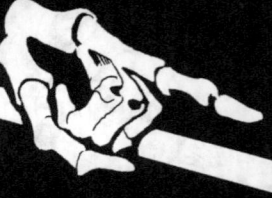

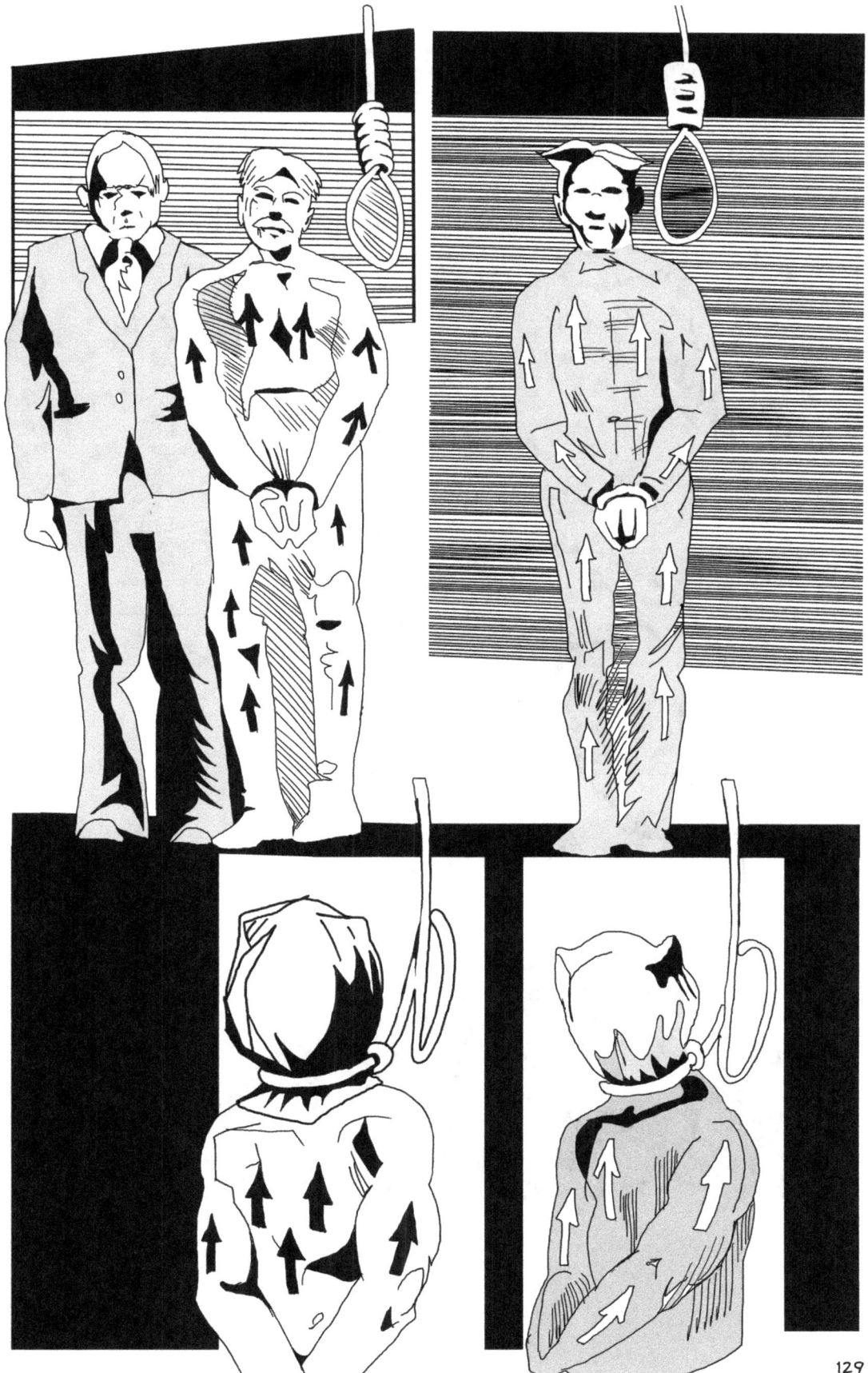

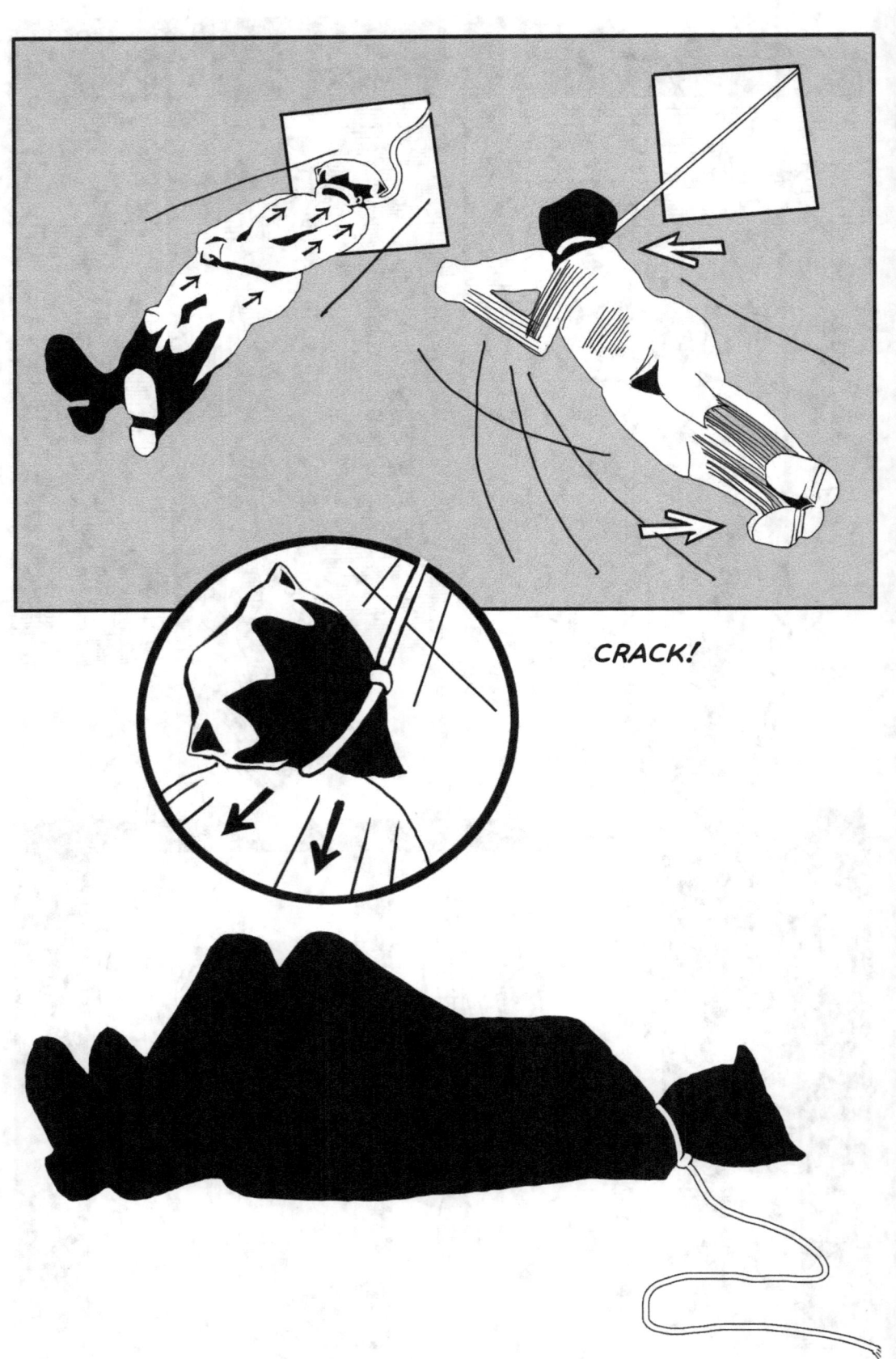

CRACK!

# ELYSIUM 6

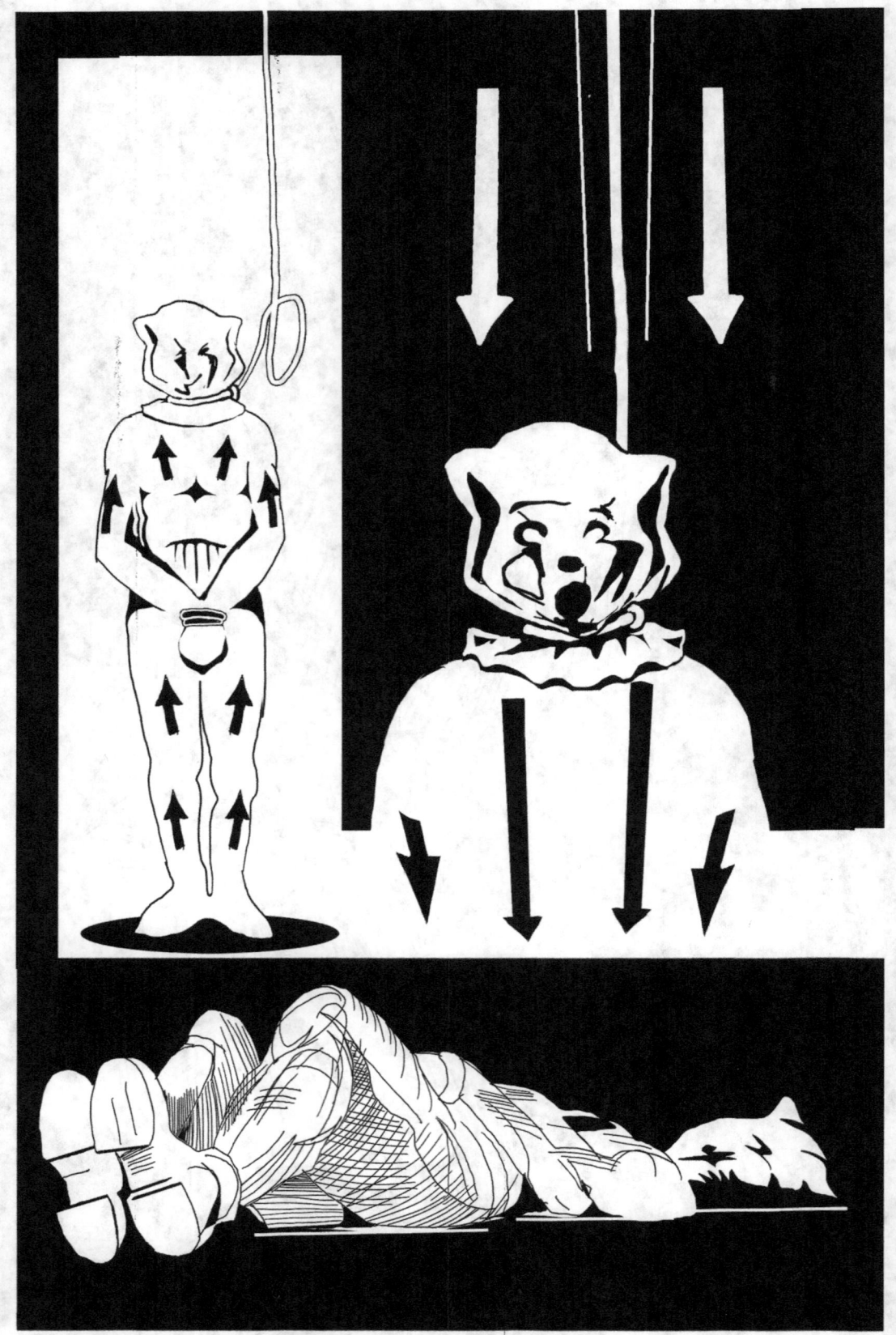

133

141

143

AT FIRST IT WAS GUNS DOWN, BUT THEN THE PALS GOT THE JUMP ON JACKO

SEEKING SHELTER, THEY BROKE FOR THE RUINED HOUSE

FIGHT DIDN'T LAST LONG -- IT WAS HOPELESS FROM THE START

146

147

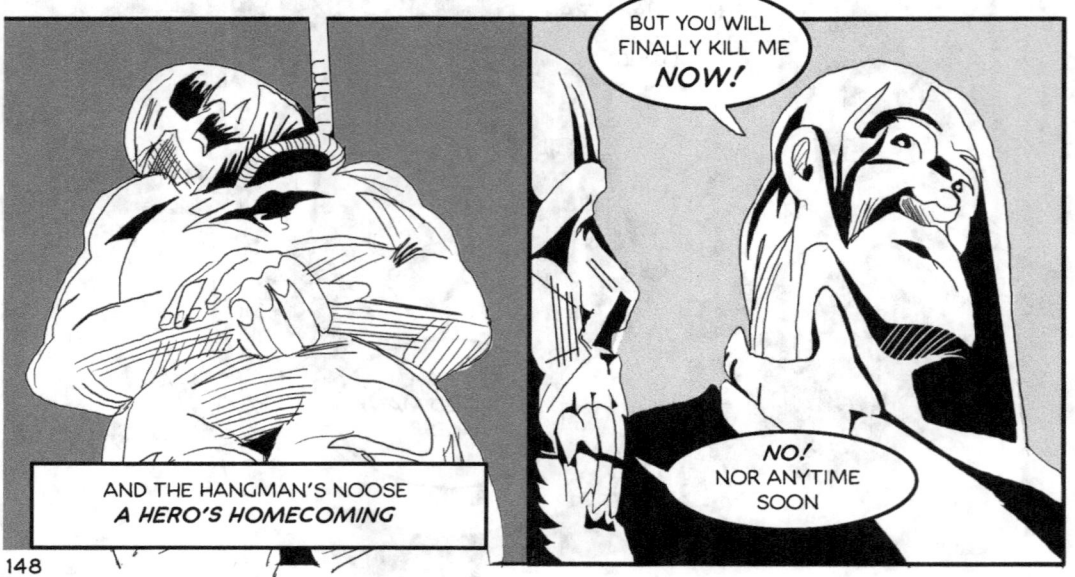

I SURVIVED THE FIGHT AT THE WALL
*MY DEATH BY EXECUTION AT WALL*

AND THE ASSAULT ON *HILL Q*

AND THE HEADSHOT *BY FRIENDLY FIRE IN THE BUSH*

*AND THE GAS OF YRES*

AND THE HANGMAN'S NOOSE
*A HERO'S HOMECOMING*

BUT YOU WILL FINALLY KILL ME *NOW!*

*NO!* NOR ANYTIME SOON

CAPTAIN BECK
ALL OF THEM
SHOT
WHOM?
NONSENSE
TAKE HIM
AWAY
I TOLD YOU HOW
YOUR PRECIOUS "PALS" DIED
OBVIOUSLY WE HAVE MORE WORK
TO DO BEFORE YOU ARE
RELEASED
HE IS STILL HERE

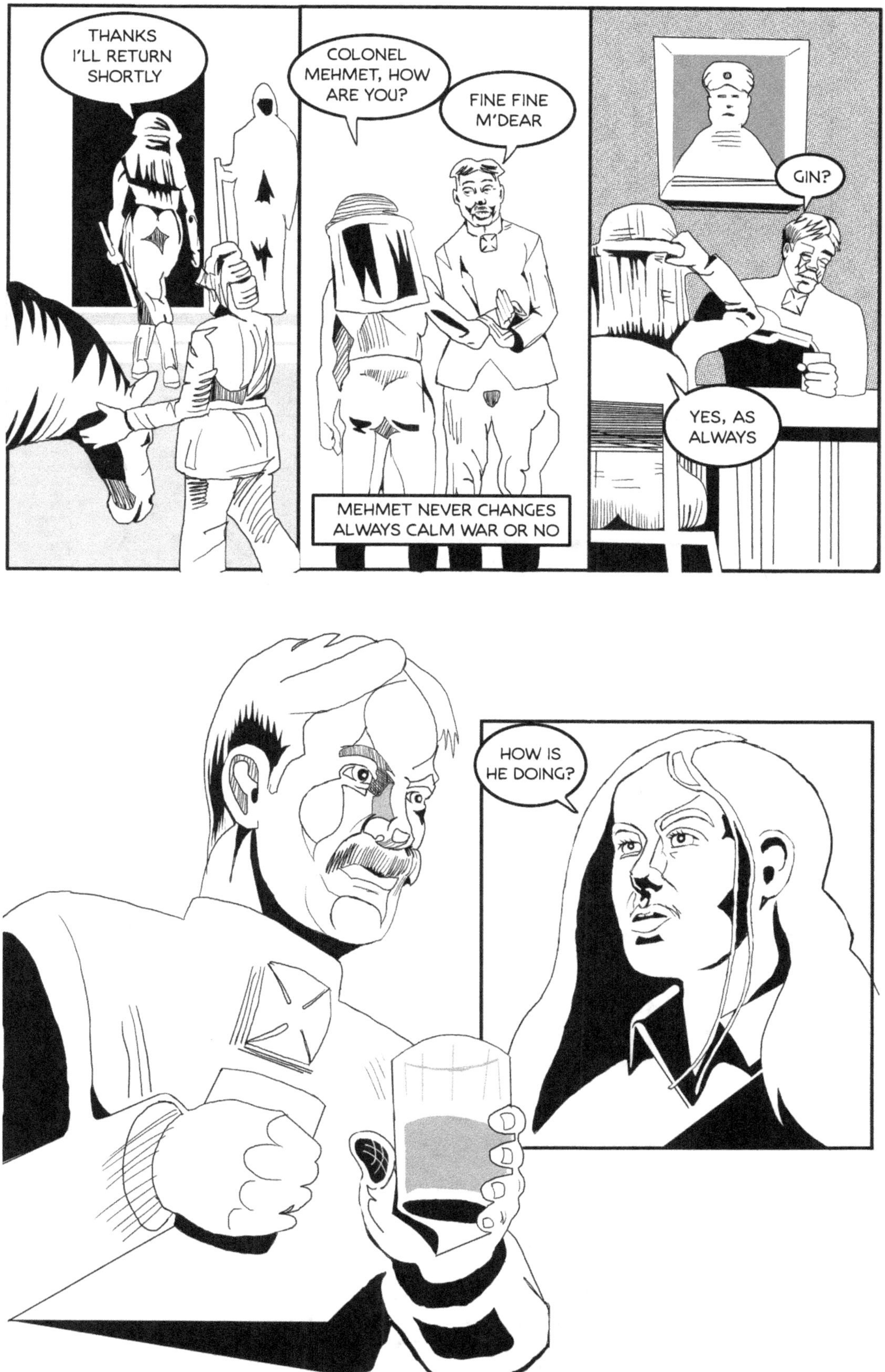

151

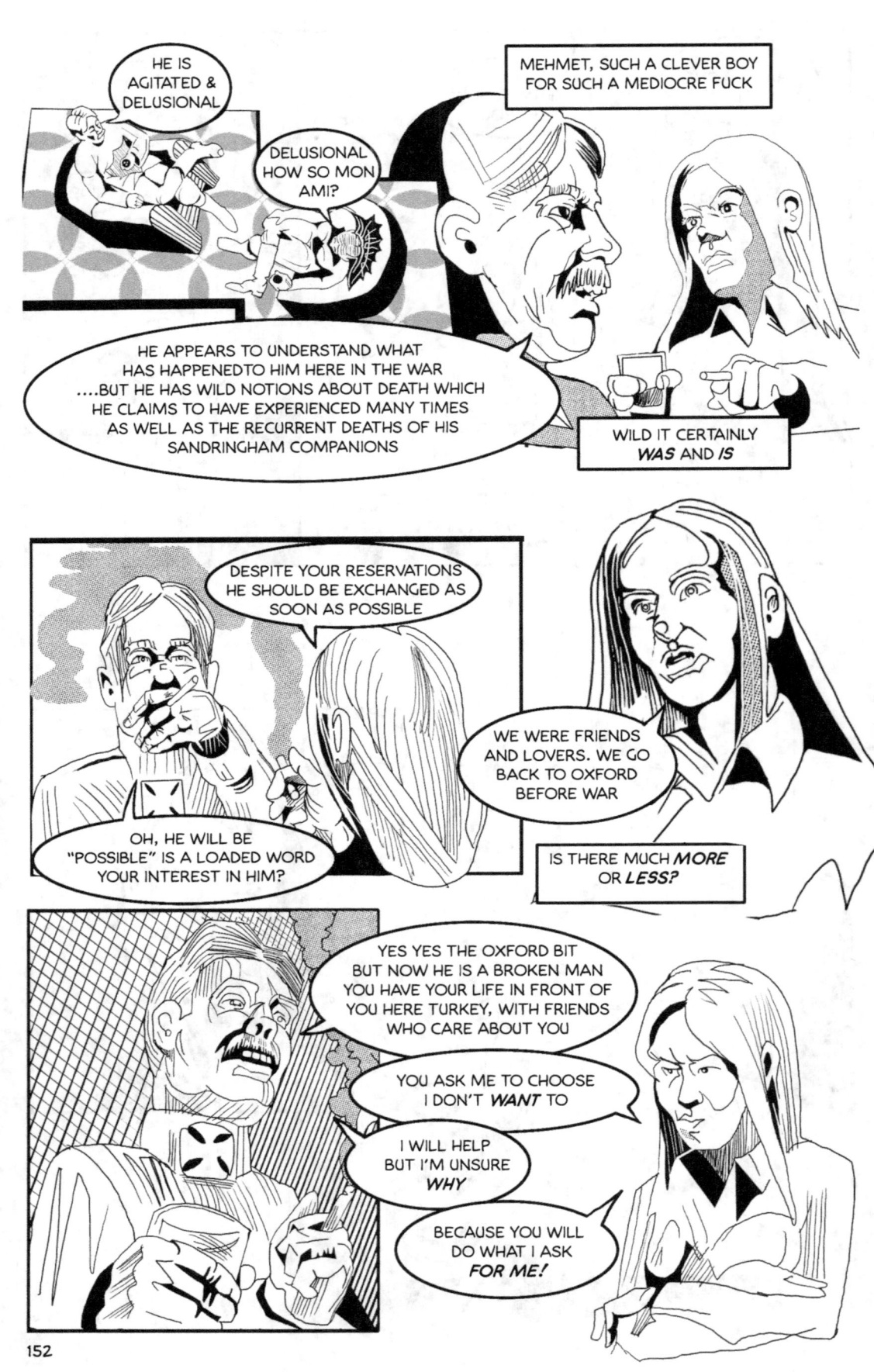

153

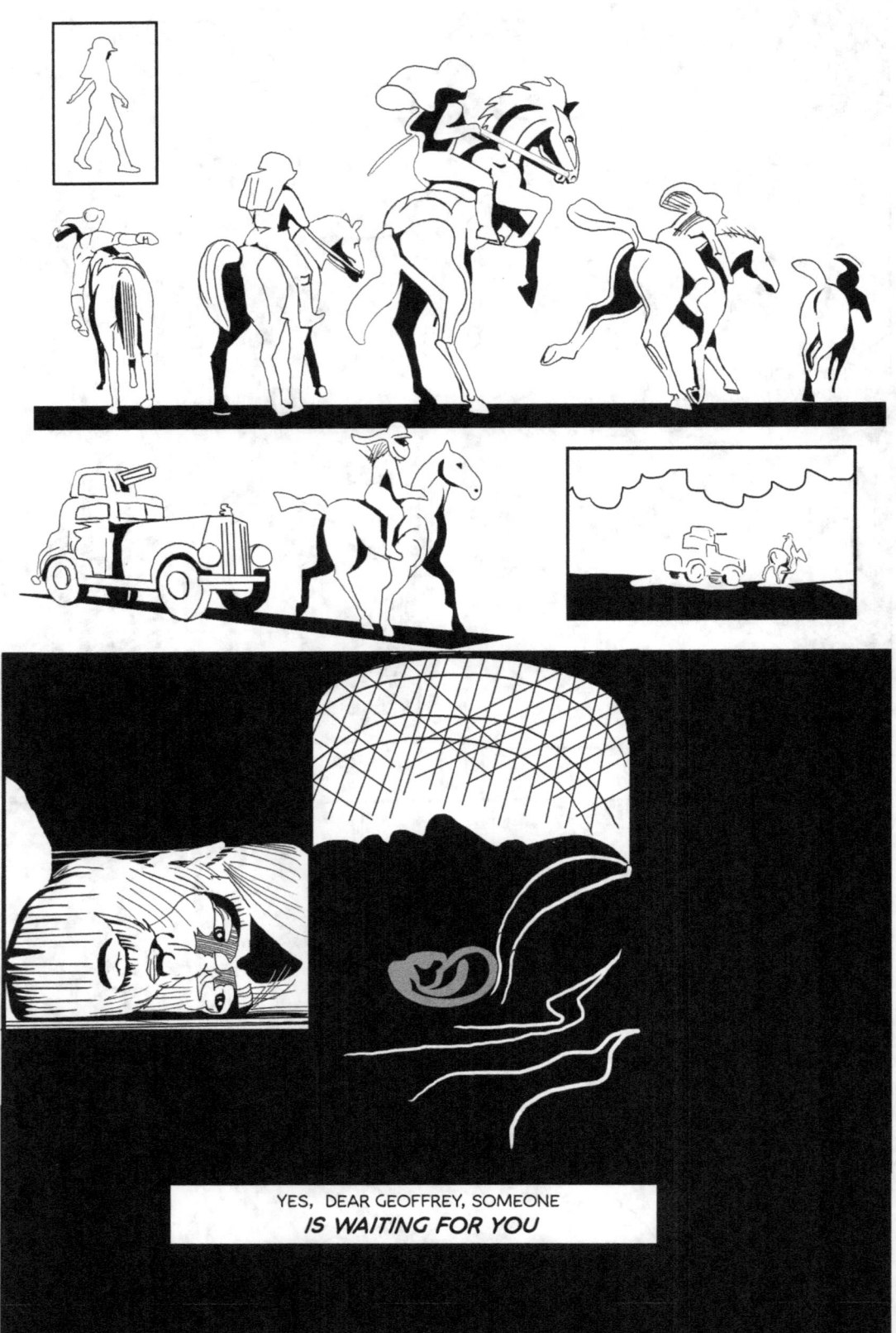

YES, DEAR GEOFFREY, SOMEONE
*IS WAITING FOR YOU*

# ARTIST'S NOTES
## (SPOILER ALERT)

*TUZAGI* MAKES USE OF ANIMAL IMAGERY TO VISUALLY EXPRESS THE POETIC NOTIONS OF METAPHOR, EPITHET AND SIMILE. THE INSPIRATION HERE IS OBVIOUSLY *HOMERIC EPIC, FOR* BOTH STORY AND DESCRIPTIVE TECHNIQUE. OUR MAIN CHARACTERS, *GEOFFREY BEGOLE-SMITH* AND *HELEN DOUGHTY-WYLIE* ARE OFTEN SEEN IN THEIR METAPHORIC FORMS, RESPECTIVELY, OF THE *BRITISH BULL MASTIFF* AND THE *RED DEER HART.* THEIR ANIMAL FORMS , THE METAPHORS, RECREATE IN ACTION A VISUAL NOTION OF THE *HOMERIC SIMILE.*

THE BRITISH BULL DOG IS A RELATIVELY RECENT ICON, HAVING EMERGED IN THE 19TH CENTURY AS THE BOSOM COMPANION OF JOHN BULL, THE ENGLISH "UNCLE SAM"; IN OUR STORY, WE HAVE UPGRADED HIM TO A MASTIFF, AN ANIMAL CAPABLE OF WINNING A FIGHT WITH, E.G. AN ASIAN HYENA. OUR STOUT ENGLISH CLASSICIST AND SOLDIER, GEOFFREY, IS ALL BULL MASTIFF WHEN ROUSED TO FIGHT A DESPERATE ACTION.

THE RED DEER HART, OR STAG, ON THE OTHER HAND, IS AN ICON OF GREAT ANTIQUITY, THAT MAY BE ASSOCIATED WITH EASTERN NOMADS, AND RELEVANT TO OUR STORY, THE HITTITES WHO RULED MUCH OF BRONZE AGE ANATOLIA(TURKEY). THE RED DEER IS SUGGESTIVE OF THE HITTITE GOD OF THE HUNT. SPIRITUALLY IT CONNECTS OUR HELEN, A HUNTER OF ANCIENT ARTIFACTS AND MEN, GOOD AND BAD. A VIRILE FEMALE, HELEN MUST BE A HART -- ANTLERS MATTER.

THE STORIES ALSO USE WILD DOGS, JACKALS AND ASIAN HYENAS -- EVIL SPIRITS IN DOGLIKE FORM-- TO REPRESENT THE DARKER SIDE OF MEN IN WAR, REGARDLESS THEIR NOMINAL AFFILIATIONS, ENGLISH OR TURK.

OUR VIOLENT AUSTRALIAN NCO IS LIKENED TO A MINOAN BULL*!*

IT IS THE AUTHOR/ARTIST'S HOPE THE IMAGERY IS SELF-EXPLANATORY, BUT SOME OF THE ABRUPT TRANSITIONS IN THE STORIES MAY BE CONFUSING.

# REFERENCES
## "HOW TO BOOKS"

THE FOLLOWING IS A VERY SELECT LIST OF REFERENCES THAT WERE ESSENTIAL IN THEIR OWN UNIQUE WAYS TO THE COMPLETION OF *TUZAGI*.

WILLIAM II, FREDDIE. *THE D.C. COMICS GUIDE TO DIGITALLY DRAWING COMICS.* WATSON-GUPTILL. SEPTEMBER 1. 2009. ISBN-10: 0823099237. A SUPER REFERENCE FOR CREATORS WHO HAVE SOME PHOTOSHOP EXPERIENCE. FREDDIE ALSO A NUMBER OF ADOBE™ ADD-ON "TOOLS" THAT CUT TO THE CHASE FOR DIGITAL COMICS ARTISTS. THERE ARE A NUMBER OF "D.C. COMICS GUIDES" COVERING THE GAMUT OF RELEVANT TOPICS, FROM WRITING TO PENCILLING TO INKING TO COLORING AND LETTERING. I HAVE STUDIED THEM ALL CAREFULLY AND FOUND THEM *ESSENTIAL!*

MARTINBROUGH, SHAWN. *HOW TO DRAW NOIR COMICS: THE ART AND TECHNIQUE OF VISUAL STORYTELLING.* WATSON-GUPTILL. 1ST EDITION OCTOBER 30, 2007. ISBN-13: 978-0823024-06-3. GREAT INSTRUCTION ON HOW TO PUT B&W IMAGES TOGETHER TO TELL A STORY.

LOWE, JOHN. *WORKING METHODS: COMIC CREATORS DETAIL THEIR STORYTELLING AND ARTISITIC PROCESSES.* TWOMORROWS PUBLISHING. MAY 2007. ISBN-13: 978-1-893905-73-3. A WONDERFUL LOOK AT HOW A NUMBER OF INDUSTRY PROFESSIONALS EACH TAKE A SHORT SCRIPT AND PRODUCE A FINISHED PIECE OF SEQUENTIAL ART.

RAVEN, FIONA & GLENNA COLLETT. *BOOK DESIGN MADE SIMPLE.* 12 PINES PRESS. 2016. ISBN-13: 978-0-9940969-0-6. "A STEP BY STEP GUIDE TO DESIGNING AND TYPESETTING YOUR OWN BOOK IN ADOBE™ INDESIGN".

## SHORT BIBLIOGRAPHY

MCCRERY, NIGEL. *ALL THE KING'S MEN.* SIMON&SHUSTER UK. 1992. ISBN-10: 0-671-01831-0. THE STANDARD ACCOUNT OF THE 1/5 NORFOLK AT GALLIPOLI. THE BOOK WAS THE BASIS FOR A VERY GOOD BBC PRODUCTION OF THE SAME NAME.

CARLYON, L.A. *GALLIPOLI.* DOUBLEDAY. 2002. ISBN-10: 0-385-60475-0. GOOD GENERAL HISTORY OF THE CAMPAIGN FROM THE AUSTRALIAN PERSPECTIVE. THERE IS A LARGE AND GROWING LITERATURE ON THE SUBJECT, CARLYON IS A GOOD PLACE TO START.

CHAMBERS, STEPHEN. *SUVLA: AUGUST OFFENSIVE.* PEN&SWORD BOOKS LTD. 2011. ISBN-13: 978-1-84884-543-5. A BRIEF, BUT DETAILED MILITARY HISTORY OF THE AUGUST OFFENSIVE.

ERICKSON, EDWARD J. *GALLIPOLI: THE OTTOMAN CAMPAIGN.* PEN&SWORD BOOKS LTD. 2010. ISBN-13: 978-1-84415-967-3. GALLIPOLI FROM "THE OTHER SIDE OF THE FENCE". BASED ON TURKISH SOURCES.

THE AUSTRALIAN, BRITISH, AND NEW ZEALAND *OFFICIAL HISTORIES.* THE BRITISH OH IS THE EASIEST TO READ, WITH VERY GOOD MAPS. THE AUSTRALIAN OH IS VERY MUCH A SPECIALIST'S READ.